PRAISE AN[

PLEASE LEAVE AN ONLINE BOOK REVIEW

Book reviews are the lifeblood of authors. Your review will encourage me to write more fantasy novels for your enjoyment, and it makes this more of a conversation.

Book awards and 5-star reviews from:

- Readers' Choice Book Awards: Best Teen Book, 2023
- Pinnacle Book Achievement Awards: Fantasy, Gold Award Winner, 2023
- Outstanding Creator Awards: Teen and Young-Adult (YA), Winner, 2023
- #1 New Release: Amazon, Children's Fantasy & Magic Adventure
- Literary Titan Book Award: Fantasy, Gold Award Winner, 2023

"With a unique and imaginative plot, a mesmerising magical multiverse, and a host of wonderful and magical creatures, this book will appeal to young adult readers who enjoy adventure and fantasy fiction. A fun, fantasy fiction novel, packed full of magic and adventure. A thrilling ride through the multiverse, not to be missed!"

- Readers' Choice, 5-star review

"A captivating tale that follows the enthralling journey of siblings Ana and Zackary through a wondrous and magical Multiverse. ... Aurora Winter's talent for weaving a captivating narrative, brimming with imaginative realms and well-crafted characters, makes *Magic, Mystery, and the Multiverse* an absolute must-read for any lover of the genre."

- Literary Titan, 5-star review

"In this debut YA fantasy series-starter, Earth-born siblings find themselves stranded in a parallel world that suffers under a fiendish ruler's reign. ...Winter's opening installment showcases a colorful primary cast—particularly Ana and Zackary, who make a superb duo."

- Kirkus Reviews

"Set to be a modern classic."
   - Danielle Chritchley, 5-star Amazon review

"A fun romp the whole family will enjoy."
   - Wendy Winter, author, Where's My Joey?

"Aurora Winter combines many fantasy and sci-fi elements into a rich tapestry. The result is a swift-paced adventure story, portal-hopping across three worlds, encountering denizens both benign and malevolent. My favorites were the talking dog (that only Ana can understand), Egor, and the villain that I loved to hate. Fasten your seat belt and get ready for an exciting ride!"
   - Timothy Forner, author, Montgomery Schnauzer, PI

"I could barely put it down and I want more please! Recommended."
   - Andrea Viner, 5-star Goodreads review

"A masterpiece!"
   - Kelly Sullivan-Walden, author, I Had The Strangest Dream

"Fans of fantasy novels are in for a scrumptious treat with *Magic, Mystery and the Multiverse*. Full of characters you quickly come to love, Aurora Winter's storytelling will keep you on the edge of your seat until the very end. It's *Harry Potter* meets *Doctor Who!*"

- Michael Stockham, bestselling author, Confessions of an Accidental Lawyer

"Engaging until the very last page! Wanting more!"

- Audrey L. White, 5-star Goodreads review

"In this "superb" series starter (*Kirkus Reviews*), aspiring actress Ana and her brother, Zackary, stumble into a parallel universe where she's inundated with new friends, instant enemies, and baffling mysteries. When Zackary is kidnapped, Ana will do whatever it takes to rescue him — all while unraveling the impossible truth about her family."

- Bookbub

THANK YOU FOR YOUR REVIEW!

Thank you in advance for taking a moment to leave a starred review on Amazon, Bookbub, Goodreads, or wherever you get books. I really appreciate it!

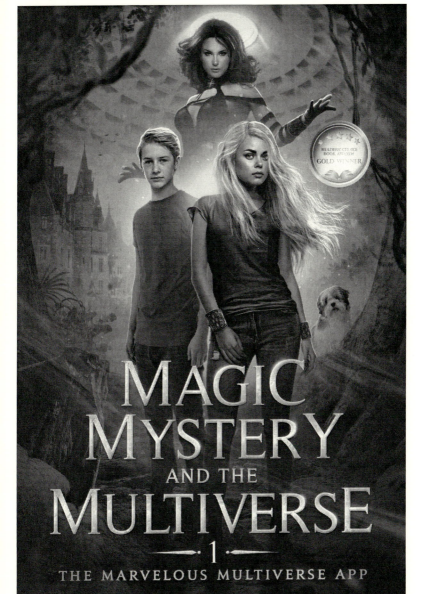

Magic, Mystery and the Multiverse

THE MARVELOUS MULTIVERSE APP

AURORA M. WINTER

Magic, Mystery and the Multiverse: The Marvelous Multiverse App
Book 1: Magic, Mystery and the Multiverse
Copyright © 2023 by Aurora Winter
All rights reserved.
Softcover ISBN 978-1-951104-22-1
Hardcover ISBN: 978-1-951104-26-9
e-book ISBN 978-1-951104-20-7
Cover design by Twin Art Design
Author photos by Jana Marcus
Maps by Yale Winter
V08252023
Publication Date: August 17, 2023
Publisher: Same Page LLC
www.SamePagePublishing.com

No part of this book may be reproduced in any form or by any electronic or mechanical means, including information storage and retrieval systems, without written permission from the author, except for the use of brief quotations in a book review.

For my mother, who believed even when I didn't.

CONTENTS

1. Imprisoned — 1
2. The Executioner — 7
3. Magic & Choices — 14
4. Arrival — 22
5. Wish Upon A Star — 30
6. Code Breaker — 35
7. The Marvelous Multiverse App — 43
8. Crash Landing — 48
9. Murderers! — 57
10. The Cruel Queen — 61
11. Heroes — 69
12. Animal Whisperer — 74
13. Death by Prophecy — 81
14. The Gossipfly — 88
15. Disguises — 93
16. Off to Bluebells Inn — 100
17. Veto's Superpowers — 105
18. Veto Warns of Danger — 114
19. How Do You Make a Puppet? — 118
20. We've Got to Get Out of Here — 126
21. Meeting Marilla — 131
22. What's Behind That Door? — 137
23. Save the Cat — 143
24. The Secret Multiverse Academy — 149
25. In the Cellar — 156
26. Puppet #2 — 160
27. A Magical Mistake — 167
28. Room #33 — 175
29. The Portal — 180

30. The Ghastly Garden	185
31. Illegal Alien	190
32. Run, Ana, Run!	196
33. A Noble Sacrifice	202
34. Prince Hunter	204
35. The Portal	206
36. Divas	210
37. Arrested	215
38. You're My Only Hope	221
39. The Choice	229
40. The Reluctant Spy	235
Book 2: The Secret Multiverse Academy (Bonus Chapter)	244
Acknowledgments	252
Aurora M. Winter	255
Get the series!	256

CHAPTER 1
IMPRISONED

When Ana activated the Marvelous Multiverse app to go for a joyride, she never imagined it would mean her death. She was sentenced to burn at the stake this very morning. It had been fun exploring this parallel universe—until everything went horribly wrong and the Crimson Censor had framed Ana for Word Crimes ... and murder.

Ana Zest had never been in a worse fix. She had lost the Parallel Universe Pod (PUP)—and lost her brother. Her brother would die if she didn't rescue him soon. But first, she had to rescue herself.

I have to free my hands before the guards come back!

Ana focused on sawing through the thick hemp rope that bound her hands behind her back. She rubbed the rope against a sharp corner on the frame of her narrow prison bed. Dirty metal bands encircled her wrists like shackles. The friction wore the dust and grime away, revealing a glint of copper or gold. The metal bands weren't shackles, but bracelets embellished with mysterious runes.

One slender thread of the thick rope snapped and curled free.

The light slanting through the prison bars gradually increased as the moonlight from two moons gave way to dawn breaking. Time was running out! Ana redoubled her efforts to saw through the rope.

She had to save herself, and then save her brother. She wasn't on Earth.

No Wi-Fi, no cell towers. No phone, no way to call for help.

No one knows where I am. No one's coming to save me.

There is nothing like imminent death to focus the mind. Of course, what the mind fixated on was ... death.

Is that smoke? Have they already lit the bonfire?

Ana clambered up onto the bed frame and peered out the high, barred window set in the stone walls. Dawn broke, and the sun threatened to emerge from behind the mountains. Sunrise meant death. She detected a hint of smoke, which caught in her throat and made her cough.

She stood on tiptoe and peered over the

windowsill, trying to see the bonfire flames. Instead, she was confronted by a spider. Reacting with primal fear, Ana dropped to the floor with a gasp.

Get a grip on yourself. The spider is the least of your troubles.

Ana returned to the critical task of freeing her hands. She scratched the rope against the corroded iron bed frame. Rust flaked off as her hands became numb. Unseen, the spider let out a nearly invisible thread and dropped into Ana's long hair. Ana rubbed the rope against the rusty bed frame.

Another slender thread broke and snaked free.

Sweat trickled down her brow, and Ana wiped her head against her shoulder. She blinked several times to rehydrate her blue contact lenses, which were gritty and irritating.

Ana had stunning violet eyes. Coupled with her long white hair, her unusual appearance attracted attention. But she had years of practice avoiding unwanted attention. With colored contact lenses to make her eyes appear blue or brown, and dye to change her hair color, she could appear normal. At least in California.

People look—but they do not see. If you give them something memorable to notice, that's all they recall. That could be useful, especially in Hollywood. She was an actor. Not famous yet, but she'd had a few gigs.

Ana Zest was a chameleon. She could pass for an

alluring young woman by adding makeup, heels, a push-up bra, a wig, and a sexy dress. It was all about energy. It was the hip-swaying walk, the sultry energy she could choose to project. But ditch all that, add overalls and a baseball cap, she looked like a boy. Add a fake tattoo and a nose ring, and that was what people recalled. Or she could appear to be a responsible teenager when she wore her school uniform of a white blouse and plaid skirt.

Give people a new look, a new name, a new attitude, and she became someone new. People remembered the window dressing.

Becoming a chameleon had begun innocently enough, with colored contacts. Her father insisted she camouflage her violet eyes. Why was he ashamed of her?

No! Don't think about that. Focus, Ana, focus!

Ana continued vigorously sawing the hemp rope against the rough surface. Her wrists were getting raw, but she was making progress. The rope gave an inch. Hope—that most precious feeling—flooded her.

But at that moment, she heard footsteps. Two prison guards arrived, crushing her hopes and curdling the acid in her stomach. One was a red-bearded dwarf, the other a skinny human with a shifty, sneaky attitude.

"Zorana Zest. Time to meet yer executioner," said

the dwarf. Keys jingled as he unlocked the iron door to her cell.

The guards entered, and the shifty one noticed the chafed rope. "Hey! Dat's destruction of prison property, dat is."

"Stolen property, that is," said the dwarf, eying her bracelets with greed. He wiped his thick thumb across the layer of grime on the cuff, revealing ancient runes and tiny emeralds. The mysterious metal gleamed, hinting that it might be gold. "What's made by dwarfs belongs to dwarfs. Everyone knows that."

The skinny guard glanced over his shoulder to make sure no one was watching their skulduggery. "No sense melting 'em in the fire. Doin' ya a favor, really."

"You'll be sorry," Ana warned.

The shifty guard tried to yank a magical cuff off of Ana's wrist, but it zapped him with a nasty electric shock. "Ow! Opus Die, that hurt."

"Stop monkeying around." The dwarf grabbed Ana's wrist and tried to unbuckle one of the mysterious cuffs. He was rewarded with an even stronger electric jolt that threw him against the cell wall. His hair and eyebrows stood on end, and the air sizzled with the smell of burned hair. Horrified, he said, "They're enchanted!"

"I did warn you. They won't come off while I'm alive," Ana said.

"Well … that won't be for much longer. We'll have 'em off ya soon enough." The shifty guard roughly secured her hands behind her back with a fresh rope.

"But the fire will destroy the cuffs. The gold will melt!" the red-bearded dwarf protested.

"We can still sell the gold, even if it's a twisted lump," said the shifty guard.

"But the executioner won't—"

"Shut yer trap," warned the shifty guard.

The frustrated guards shoved Ana out of her prison cell and toward her doom.

CHAPTER 2
THE EXECUTIONER

Ana's heart pounded like thundering horse's hooves as the prison guards shoved her roughly forward.

A hint of smoke laced the air. Wood had been piled around a pole, ready to consume its victim in flames. The townspeople of Prosperus, Tellusora, didn't want to miss this morning's entertainment, so they had gathered to watch the show.

Standing on the raised platform, the executioner addressed the onlookers. "This witch has been sentenced to die for her crimes. Miss Zorana Zest is guilty of Word Crimes, theft of property, kidnapping Marilla Berger—"

"I did not!" Ana protested.

"Hold your tongue, witch," growled the red-bearded dwarf.

The executioner continued addressing the crowd. "And the worst crime of all ... murder."

The crowd gasped with horrified delight.

Won't there be a stay of execution? Things always work out. Don't they?

Time seemed to slow down. Ana was aware of the sound of her own breath accompanying the throbbing of her heartbeat. She hummed quietly as she rubbed the thick rope against the metal cuffs, desperately trying to free her bound wrists.

"No burnin' today," announced the executioner.

The crowd grumbled.

What was that? Hope sprang up, as perky and resilient as a dandelion weed.

"No fires allowed. Too risky. On account of all the wildfires. So we'll have to settle for an old-fashioned hangin'."

A noose of thick hemp rope dangled ominously from the hangman's pole. The guards shoved Ana underneath it.

"You're a lucky girl. Hangin' is quick and easy compared to burnin'. Your prayers were answered," said the executioner.

If my prayers were answered, I would get out of this, find my brother, find the PUP, and go home.

"Don't be worried none," said the executioner. "They don't call me One-Jerk Jerry for nothin'. One and done. It'll be over before you know it."

Desperate for deliverance, Ana scanned the crowd. But she didn't see anyone about to rescue her. Instead, she saw a crowd eager for a show. She chewed on her lip, realizing that she was this morning's entertainment.

Suddenly, a magnificent coach pulled up, drawn by two sleek dapple-gray horses. The coach had a distinctive crest: a slash over a circle with a pointy tail, like a crossed-out speech bubble, the symbol of Opus Die. A captain attired in a crisp gray uniform opened the carriage door, and out stepped the Crimson Censor—Brightness Cacophony. This was the woman—or wicked witch—who had framed Ana for murder.

The Crimson Censor exuded power, wealth, and danger. Magnificently dressed, she wore a tight golden bodice, puffy lace sleeves evocative of a spider's web, and a red skirt that stopped mid-calf, revealing finely shaped legs and killer stiletto heels. A lustrous golden cuff adorned each wrist.

Could this be a last-minute reprieve? Ana wondered, ever hopeful.

Ana searched the Crimson Censor's face for a flicker of softness. But Crimson's regal face was hard, cold, and cruel. Her ivory skin was translucent, her wasp waist tiny, her hair crimson to match her name. Crimson hated Ana, and she was the reason Ana was about to die. She said something to the captain, who nodded and marched purposefully toward the gallows.

She's ordered a stay of execution, right? Just in the nick of time!

"Stand here." Jerk pushed Ana to stand on the dreaded trapdoor.

Nestled in Ana's long white hair, the spider observed as Jerk placed the rough hemp rope around her neck.

"That itches," complained Ana.

"Not for long," said Jerk.

"Wait a minute, wait a minute! Don't I get the last word?" Ana stalled frantically.

"Very unlikely you'll get *the* last word." Jerk chuckled at his gallows humor. "But you can say *your* last words. That's always a crowd-pleaser."

The crowd murmured in curious anticipation. Meanwhile, the captain pushed his way woodenly through the throng.

Ana worried at the hemp rope tying her wrists behind her back, and one slender thread curled free.

"Give them a show," she whispered, talking to herself to rein in her fear. "My last words ... my last words ... a sure crowd-pleaser ... likely get applause ... maybe even tips for the executioner."

Jerk carefully snugged the noose carefully around her neck.

The captain plowed through the crowd. His gray

uniform bore the insignia of Opus Die, and that made people move aside.

Ana scanned his face, but found nothing but the lifeless and emotionless expression of a plank of wood, as cold and hard as the surface of a bronze sculpture. Unmoved by compassion, not even a glimmer of feeling shone on his rigid wooden features.

"Hang on a minute! Look there—he has something to say." Ana jerked her chin toward the approaching captain.

"Ya got somethin' to say, Captain Koercer?" Jerk called out.

"The Crimson Censor says get on with it," the Koercer captain shouted robotically. "It is past dawn. You are behind schedule."

What?! No last-minute reprieve? Ana thought, incredulous.

Ana's heart dropped into her stomach with a nauseating lurch. Her mouth went dry and tasted of copper. She desperately rubbed the golden cuffs against the rope securing her wrists behind her back.

Like a rat fleeing a sinking ship, the spider scuttled up the nearby post.

Jerk harrumphed. "Ain't my fault about the wildfires and change of plans to a hangin'."

"Why not wait until tomorrow?" Ana suggested.

Jerk snorted, amused.

"Are them your last words?" Jerk asked.

"No, no, no … give me a minute," Ana pleaded.

But Ana's showmanship skills chose this moment to abandon her. She was at a loss. Her mouth was dry. Her usually nimble brain had shut down. Fight, flight, or freeze. She couldn't fight, she couldn't flee. So her brain opted to freeze just when she needed it the most.

"Come on, I haven't got all day, Zorana," grumbled Jerk.

"Uh …" said Ana.

Jerk announced to the crowd, "And the last words of the convicted criminal Miss Zorana Zest are …" He glared at her meaningfully. "Time's up."

Could this really be it? Everyone has to die one day. I guess this is my day.

Finally, Ana spoke. "I commend my soul to the care of my mother's angel and to God. May I be forgiven for my sins, and may God bless my brother and free him from evil and illness. So be it. So it is."

The spider dangled from the wooden beam overhead, waving its legs as if to say goodbye. Its nearly invisible web suspended it like a marionette hanging from strings. The spider dropped onto her shoulder.

"Them's good last words." Jerk nodded approvingly.

He put a burlap bag over Ana's face. Boards creaked as he stepped away and pulled the lever, which groaned. The trapdoor fell open with a click.

Gravity claimed her. Ana Zest fell with a sickening lurch.

Her body came to a sudden stop in midair as it reached the end of the hangman's noose, then bounced a little. Her legs windmilled wildly, then stilled. Inside the burlap bag, the curious spider crawled on her face, which surely would have made her scream ... but it was too late for screaming.

CHAPTER 3
MAGIC & CHOICES

Consciousness arose like a gray whale emerging from the depths.

Where am I? Am I dead? Is this heaven?

Groggily regaining consciousness, Ana sensed she was not alone.

"Ah ... I see you're back in the land of the living," said an unfamiliar, refined voice.

I'm alive? I'm alive! Ana couldn't believe her good luck. *See, things always work out.*

She fought to blink open one crusty eyelid, and then the other. Before her stood someone who looked more like a vampire than an angel. *Definitely not heaven, then.*

"So glad you could join us, Miss *Zorana Zest*. Or should I call you Miss *Ana*?"

How does he know I go by Ana? I told everyone here

that my name was Zorana. Ana jolted upright. That proved to be a mistake. Her sudden movement triggered a pounding headache, as if the sharp beak of an incessant woodpecker was pecking her head. She groaned.

Ana's bruised throat was swollen and tender, so it hurt to swallow. She tried to speak, but managed only a dusty croak. She discovered she was sitting on a reclined armchair with many levers, possibly one used by dentists. Or torturers.

Her eyes swept the room, taking in the elegant, spacious study. This was no jail cell, and an ember of hope sparked to life in her stubbornly optimistic heart. A servant hovered nearby, attentive yet unobtrusive. Not quite human, he was tall, lean, and quiet as a shadow. Dark, greasy hair framed his rectangular face like limp curtains.

She blinked owlishly, struggling to remember. Hadn't she seen him before? She felt discombobulated.

Her eyes returned to the dignified, slender man sitting behind the mahogany desk, toying with a sharp letter opener. His piercing gaze seemed to see right through her, to what she had eaten for breakfast, her private resentments, and her secret dreams. His exterior was cool, calculating, and in control, but she had the impression of barely contained lethal ferocity behind that facade. He was dressed in black, which made her think of vampires. Probably he wasn't a vampire—more likely a politician.

Ana rubbed her dry eyes. Her blue contact lenses fell out, revealing her unusual violet eyes. Her fragile contact lenses stuck to her hand like shriveled blue petals from a forget-me-not. One was torn, the other ragged.

"Do give our guest some tea, Egor," instructed the man with a wave of his long elegant fingers. His manicured hands were those of a pianist, not the hands of a man who worked with machinery—unless it was the machinery of people, politics, and power. "And do see about rehydrating her contact lenses."

Egor moved to obey.

"Let me introduce myself. I am Lord Orator. Your amnesia is a temporary side effect of your near-death experience. It will pass as blood flow returns to your brain."

Lord Orator was obviously important, rich, and powerful, but was he a friend or an enemy? Suddenly aware that she must appear disheveled and discombobulated, she sat up demurely.

Appearance matters! You can never convince anyone of anything looking like a bedraggled mess.

Ana finger-combed the tangles in her long white hair, disturbing the hitchhiker spider. It waved its thin legs in the air, but no one noticed it.

A lapdog slept on his bed by the fire, one brown leg

contrasting oddly with the rest of his white and tan fur. Egor poured tea from the teapot, added several generous spoonfuls of honey, then brought her the steaming mug.

"Drink. Let me take thothe," Egor lisped. His calloused hands picked up her shriveled blue contact lenses with surprising care. He popped them into a vial that he had taken from his pocket.

She sipped the warm black tea. It tasted of honey, cinnamon, cloves, and something else she couldn't quite place. Orange rind? She inhaled the clove-scented steam, and it helped her to breathe more easily.

Her whole body hurt, as if she had whiplash from a car accident. Her head pounded. Her throat felt as if someone had taken sandpaper to the inside and a sledgehammer to the outside. It would be foolish to make any sudden moves. She wasn't capable of making a run for it. Not yet, anyway. Her legs were like jelly. There was no strength in them. She sipped more of the honeyed tea, grateful that it soothed her raw throat.

"I wish to speak to you about magic." Lord Orator put down the letter opener and steepled his hands.

"Magic?" Ana croaked. Despite the tea, her words came out like a dusty lump of charcoal that spoiled the pristine energy of Lord Orator's stately office. Her tongue was swollen inside her mouth like a bulky foreign object. It was like talking with a mouth full of frogs.

"Drink some more tea. It will make you feel better," said Lord Orator.

Ana sipped the tea, wondering how she had survived.

As if reading her thoughts, Lord Orator answered her unspoken question. "Mr. Jerry is a precision craftsman who has turned hanging into a precise science. It's about weight and velocity and temperature. The thickness of the rope, the precise placement, the pressure points, the arteries. And most of all, timing. Timing is key in all matters of state and power. Timing is key in all matters of life and death. A few seconds can be decisive. More than a hundred people saw Miss Zorana die. Perception is reality."

Ana blinked, dizzy with his words. She rubbed her tender throat. "Thank you for saving my life?"

She hasn't meant to sound so tentative. Everything about this audience with Lord Orator suggested that her life was still hanging by a thread—and that he held the scissors. As if to underscore that point, a pair of sharp scissors graced the top of his polished mahogany desk. Lord Orator fussed with the scissors, aligning them neatly with the silver letter opener.

"Mr. Jerry does fine work. Life or death is dictated by the kind of noose, the placement of the knot, the elasticity of the rope, the weight of the subject. A knot can appear to be a hangman's noose—yet not tighten all the way. But your secret salvation was in the elasticity of the invisible second rope, thanks to my little spy. A stroke of genius, if I do say so myself." The tiniest hint of a smile flashed across Lord Orator's face. "Otherwise, your fate would have been more of a coin toss. I prefer to stack the odds in my favor."

Ana's brow furrowed. "The spider?"

"The SpyDer works for me. Speaking of which, where is that SpyDer?" Lord Orator asked Egor.

Egor examined Ana, discovered the SpyDer, and gently removed it from Ana's tangled hair. "Got it, my Lord. I thould have theen it earlier, but ith tho tiny ith practically invithible."

"Every asset is also a liability," Lord Orator mused philosophically. "But ... every liability is also an asset. The yin and yang of the universe."

Egor examined the mechanical SpyDer, then clicked it off. "Out of elastic K-lar thread. I will refill it."

"Mmm," agreed Lord Orator.

"You saved me? But why?" Ana asked. "I mean, thank you and everything, my lord, but ..."

Lord Orator turned his intense gaze on Ana, and she squirmed. "I have questions. You have answers. I saved your life. I believe the least you can do to thank me is provide answers."

"Mmm."

"Egor, bring out the Manifester."

Egor unlocked a cabinet, brought out a small box, and placed the Manifester on a round table beside Ana. He opened the box, revealing a tarantula the size of a man's hand.

Ana gasped and shrank back. "I hate spiders!"

"It's not a spider. That is a Manifester. Disguised as a spider."

She gulped. Lord Orator was more terrifying than the spider-Manifester thingy, but the creepy, insect-like contraption made her skin crawl.

"With your permission?" Lord Orator asked.

Ana hesitated. "And if I refuse?"

"There is always a choice." Lord Orator waited, his thin lips a grim line.

He stroked his fussy black goatee without revealing a trace of impatience. There was something about his manner that suggested that he knew her—even if she didn't know him.

Why did he give her a choice? What did that say about him? What would be the consequences of not cooperating? Ana hesitated, her thoughts churning in turmoil. The tea had soothed her frayed nerves and relaxed her most unnaturally. What was in that tea?

She surreptitiously studied Lord Orator. His skin was pale, as if he never went outside. He was so thin she imagined he survived on dry crusts of bread and water. His high forehead was furrowed, probably from scheming and strategizing. Ana guessed he might be about the same age as her father.

After a moment of hesitation, Ana took a deep breath and decided to cooperate. He had saved her life, and she needed to stay in his good graces if she wanted to keep breathing. "All right. What do you want to know?"

"Show me how you arrived here, and why you were sentenced to die." Lord Orator clicked a remote, and the Manifester scuttled toward her on its eight hairy legs.

Ana reared back and gasped as the spider-like Manifester crabbed up her arm and onto her neck. It pricked her neck with needle legs, gaining access to her neurology. Its abdomen became a projector which shone images onto a screen. The images swirled, then coalesced into a clear picture.

CHAPTER 4
ARRIVAL

As seen in the Manifester ...
LONDON, ENGLAND, EARTH.

Twinkling lights revealed London's skyline at night as an airplane landed at Heathrow International Airport.

Ana and Zackary Zest exited the customs area, rolling a luggage cart piled with their suitcases.

Ana Zest was athletic, muscled, and suntanned. She wore jeans, her favorite black leather boots—Doc Martens—and a T-shirt emblazoned with *Hollywood, California*. She had striking, long platinum-blonde hair. Her blue eyes twinkled with curiosity and mischief.

In contrast, her younger brother, Zackary Zest, was slender and pale, with long eyelashes framing green eyes. He seemed frail and drained. A red Ferrari baseball cap covered his wispy blonde hair. His Converse high-top runners were cream colored and scuffed.

A stiffly formal chauffeur wearing a dark suit held a handwritten sign that read *Zest*.

"Are you waiting for us?" Ana asked the driver.

"Miss Zorana Zest? Master Zackary Zest?" the chauffeur said with a strong Yorkshire accent.

"That's us," Ana confirmed. "But I go by Ana."

"I'm Mr. Walker, your uncle's chauffeur and butler. Follow me please, Miss Zorana—I beg your pardon, Miss Ana—and Master Zackary Zest." The chauffeur took their luggage cart. His broad shoulders and erect bearing made Ana wonder if he had served in the military.

"I've never been called 'master' before," Zackary said, savoring the sound of it.

"Master Zackary Zest," Ana said, mimicking the chauffeur's Yorkshire accent brilliantly.

"Not bad," said Zackary.

"How long will it take to get to our uncle's place?" Ana asked.

"Thames Ditton is about a half-hour drive from here at this time of night. The Old Vicarage is near Hampton Court Palace, the home of King Henry the Eighth and his ill-fated wives. You could take a tour. Highly recommended."

"I want to see the Tower of London," said Zackary.

"Did you know that Anne Boleyn was executed there after being married to King Henry the Eighth for only three years?"

"Wicked!" Zackary said.

"I rather think it was wicked to off his wife just 'cause he'd tired of her," said Ana.

The chauffeur regaled them with the history of King Henry the Eighth and his many ill-fated wives as he led them toward the black limousine.

ANA PEERED out the car window, her eyes widening as they approached the ancient stone building of the Old Vicarage. The ivy-covered walls exuded a sense of mystery and history, while the rambling structure promised countless hidden corners to explore.

As Mr. Walker, their Yorkshire-accented chauffeur, expertly maneuvered the car past the ivy-clad stone wall, Ana couldn't help but feel a sense of anticipation. He clicked a button, and the garage door opened smoothly, revealing a modern scene that stood in stark contrast to the building's ancient exterior.

Inside the garage, a symphony of steel pipes, barrels, wires, and tools awaited their arrival. High-tech equipment lined the walls, each piece vying for attention with its sleek design and intricate craftsmanship. It was a mad scientist's haven, a workshop of wonder and invention.

The chauffeur pulled the car into the garage, parked it beside an antique Bentley, and shut the garage door.

Uncle Shockley, a middle-aged man radiating energy and curiosity, greeted them from where he stood tinkering with a sleek blue car. His wild hair, reminiscent of Einstein's, matched his wild, bushy eyebrows.

His eyes lit up, and an infectious smile spread across his face. "Zorana! Zackary! Welcome to the Old Vicarage!" he said, his voice brimming with enthusiasm.

"Uncle Shockley!" chorused the kids, tumbling out of the car.

"I go by Ana now," said Ana.

"Welcome to England, Ana, Zackary. I hope you're ready for an adventure."

Zackary's eyes widened as he took in the futuristic machinery around them. Cars were his obsession. "A hydrogen-fueled Mirai! Wow!"

"The first hydrogen-fueled car," Mr. Walker observed as he took their luggage out of the trunk (which he called "the boot").

Zackary's tone turned professorial. "Actually, the first hydrogen car was made in 1965 when Roger Billings converted a Model A Ford as his high school science fair project."

His words impressed Uncle Shockley, who waved him over. "Very good, Zackary. I see you know a little about cars."

"I know a lot about cars." Zackary eagerly slid into the passenger's seat. "Is it on?"

Uncle Shockley slid into the driver's seat, clicked the start button, and the dashboard lit up. "It is now. Quiet, isn't it?" He tossed the black key fob into the black coffee-cup holder.

"They had to add artificial sound for safety." Zackary pressed buttons, exploring the dashboard menu options.

"There's no noisy engine needed! It's got a big hydrogen-powered battery. And the best part is, the exhaust is water! So much better than burning fossil fuels. And better for the environment than electric cars. See here, I've amped up the capacity ..."

Uncle Shockley eagerly opened the hood and showed the experimental car to Zackary, who peppered him with questions about his uncle's modifications.

Ana's eyes glazed over. Unlike her brother, she had no interest in anything mechanical. But she felt a twinge of excitement as she wondered what boarding school would be like. She texted her dad to let him know they'd arrived safely at their uncle's house.

Ana tuned back in to hear her uncle saying something about a puppy. She perked up, interested. "You have a puppy?"

Uncle Shockley snorted. "Not a puppy. A PUP. P-U-P. It stands for Parallel Universe Pod. Calling it that may be wishful thinking on my part. I'm missing something, but I don't know what. It's like you can't get there from here."

"I wonder what's missing," Zackary said.

"That makes two of us."

"Can we go see Hampton Court Palace tomorrow?" asked Ana.

"Or the Tower of London?" asked Zackary.

"I'm lecturing about quantum physics at the university tomorrow. The next day, we have to go to London to get your school supplies. But we can do some sightseeing before you two head off to boarding school. Tomorrow, while Mr. Walker and I are gone, you two can make yourselves at home—but don't fool around with the experimental car," Uncle Shockley said gravely. "That's strictly off-limits."

"Of course not," said Zackary. "What's Beesneese Boarding School like? Will it be like Hogwarts?"

Uncle Shockley chuckled. "Zackary, I'm afraid Beesneese is as much like Hogwarts as you are like Harry Potter!"

"In other words, not at all." Ana laughed, the sound bubbling forth like a melody. "So no flying broomsticks or talking portraits, then?"

Uncle Shockley's gaze softened as he turned his attention to Ana. "You have the same musical laughter as your mother. You remind me so much of her."

Curiosity sparked within Ana. Her mother remained a mystery to her, her memories shrouded in a fog she longed to lift. "Uncle Shockley," she began, her voice filled with eagerness, "tell me about my mother. What was she like? I don't remember her."

A shadow crossed Uncle Shockley's face, and his expression grew somber. He sighed, as if wrestling with his thoughts. "It's high time you knew the truth about your family. But it's not for me to say."

"What do you mean? What truth?" Ana asked.

"I shouldn't have said that. Never mind. It's for Ace to say when you're old enough."

"I'm old enough now," insisted Ana. "If I'm old enough to go to boarding school in another country, five thousand miles away from home, I'm old enough to know the truth about my family."

"You could be right. But ask your dad."

"Dad's in the film business. Lies and deception are his bread and butter. What's this big secret about our family?" Ana tried—but she'd gone too far.

Uncle Shockley ignored her question and gestured toward the staircase leading to the roof. "Come on. I've got something to show you two." He bounded up the spiral staircase, his eyes twinkling eagerly once again.

"And don't forget, kids. The experimental car is strictly off-limits."

The kids nodded and followed him onto the rooftop deck. Ana glanced back at the sleek blue experimental car, wondering what the big mystery was all about.

CHAPTER 5
WISH UPON A STAR

Uncle Shockley bounded onto the rooftop deck and toward a huge telescope.

"Now, let's shift our attention to the wonders of the night sky." Uncle Shockley's enthusiasm was contagious.

Intrigued by the prospect of exploring the cosmos, Ana and Zackary followed, their anticipation mounting. The crisp night air and a vast expanse of stars greeted them. The scent of honeysuckle wafted from a rooftop garden of potted plants.

The telescope stood at the ready, its lenses pointed toward the heavens. Uncle Shockley adjusted the settings with practiced ease.

He motioned for Zackary to peer through the eyepiece. "Tonight's a great night for seeing Jupiter. It's the biggest planet in our solar system."

Ana marveled at the star-studded sky, midnight blue scattered with diamonds. "There are so many more stars than in LA!"

"There are the same *number* of stars. But there's less light pollution here, so you can see more of them."

Zackary's eyes widened in wonder as the image of Jupiter came into focus. "I see something—but it's not twinkling."

"That's Jupiter. Planets don't twinkle like stars. Atmospheric effects don't interfere as much with the light we see reflected by planets."

"My turn." Ana nudged her brother aside and peered through the lens, amazed by the closeup view of Jupiter and its rings of moons and asteroids. "Wow!"

Uncle Shockley's voice took on a reverent tone as he explained the marvels of the solar system, sharing his knowledge of the celestial bodies and their mysteries. He painted a vivid picture of the cosmos.

Ana felt a growing sense of awe as the telescope revealed hidden wonders. She sensed that the mysteries of her family were intertwined with the mysteries of the universe. Standing beneath the starlit sky, Ana yearned to uncover both.

With Uncle Shockley, a font of information and insight by her side, Ana felt optimistic. He knew things, things she wanted to know, about her family and about the cosmos. Mysteries yielded their secrets if you were persistent and curious. And if you asked the right person the right questions at the right time.

"My turn." Zackary peered through the telescope. "What about parallel universes? Do you think they're real?"

"There's quite a debate in the scientific community about that. Stephen Hawking supported the theory of parallel universes. I'm on the verge of finding out if he's right. A few more tests and tweaks, and my experimental car will be ready for a spin. Wouldn't it be something if we could visit parallel universes? It would be better than time travel! What if Earth is only one planet in a multi-dimensional multiverse?"

Suddenly, a shooting star blazed through the night sky.

"Oh—look—a shooting star! Make a wish! Make a wish!" Ana said. After a moment's silence, Ana asked her brother what he had wished for.

Zackary's voice caught as he confided, "To be heroic like Percy Jackson. You know—descendant of a Greek god? So I can face death bravely."

Ana and Uncle Shockley exchanged a worried glance.

"I thought you were in remission," said Uncle Shockley.

"He is. Zackary is getting stronger every day," Ana said, more forcefully than she had intended.

"My brother shouldn't have sent you away to

boarding school if you're not well," said Uncle Shockley.

"I'm not going back to that horrible hospital. No way," said Zackary.

"You look pale. How do you feel, Zackary?" Uncle Shockley asked.

"I'm not dead yet."

Uncle Shockley shifted uneasily, unsure how to respond to Zackary's bleak mood. He was at home with science but uncomfortable with emotions.

Ana tried to lighten the atmosphere. "He's tired from the long flight. Every day above ground is a good day, right, Zee?"

"Why? It just postpones the inevitable."

"You mustn't think like that! You have to focus on the positive. Happy thoughts, healthy body," scolded Ana.

Zackary shook his head at his sister's naïve optimism.

"I've kept you up far too long." Uncle Shockley spotted Mr. Walker hovering discreetly nearby. "Ah, Mr. Walker. Please show my niece and nephew to their rooms."

"Miss Ana, Master Zackary, right this way, please. I've taken the liberty of unpacking your suitcases."

Ana and Zackary exchanged an astounded glance as they weren't used to this kind of service. Mr. Walker gestured for the kids to follow him.

"What did you wish for, Ana, on the meteor burning up as it entered Earth's atmosphere?" Uncle Shockley asked.

"On the shooting star? I wished for a really great role. Something that stretches me as an actor. I'd love to be famous!" Ana smiled brightly. "Wouldn't it be great if everyone recognized me?"

"Would it?" He raised a wild, bushy eyebrow, bemused by her answer. "Good night, Ana, Zackary."

As they left the rooftop deck, Ana wished for answers to the questions that her father stonewalled. Why were her violet eyes such a big deal? Why did she always have to hide them with colored contact lenses? Was her father ashamed of her? What was the truth about her family? She wanted to know her own story —her own past—and then create a heroic future. She'd find a good time to ask her uncle questions.

Ana hoped the shooting star would bring her good luck ... and answers.

CHAPTER 6
CODE BREAKER

As Ana and Zackary explored the depths of the Old Vicarage, they stumbled upon a hidden gem within its walls—a magnificent library, brimming with books that seemed to hold the weight of centuries. The moment they stepped inside, the scent of old parchment and ink enveloped them, mingling with the subtle mustiness that whispered of the library's long history.

Sunlight streamed through tall, stained-glass windows, casting vibrant hues across the rows of bookshelves that stretched toward the high ceiling. The shelves were rich mahogany, their polished surfaces reflecting the warm glow of the room. Books lined the walls: ancient tomes, leather-bound classics, and modern volumes side by side.

She had intended to write in her journal, but these

books were far too tempting. Ana tucked her journal into her satchel, vowing to write in it later.

A ladder leaned against the shelves, beckoning Ana. She scampered up it and trailed her fingers along the spines, humming absent-mindedly. She marveled at the sheer variety of subjects, like quantum physics, astronomy, mathematics, history, and mythology. There was an extensive collection of science fiction, including Isaac Asimov, Ray Bradbury, and Robert Heinlein.

"Cut that out," Zackary said as he plopped down in a worn leather armchair.

"Cut what out?"

"That annoying humming."

Ana rolled her eyes, stopped humming and selected a few books to explore.

Zackary sketched, his tongue protruding from his mouth in concentration. He wore jeans, a T-shirt, a sweatshirt, and his cream-colored Converse high-tops. His wispy blonde hair trailed out from underneath his red Ferrari baseball cap. A nearby antique reading lamp on a small table cast a soft glow on his sketchbook, revealing a fantastical car design in black ink.

Ana's eyes were violet, as she wasn't wearing her colored contact lenses. She wore jeans, a T-shirt, and her favorite Doc Martens, which seemed oddly out of place in this magnificent library. She descended the ladder holding several books, then peered out the window and frowned at the drizzle. "Rain. I miss LA already."

"I like rain. It suits my mood."

Ana peered at Zackary's sketch. "What's that?"

"My casket." Zackary showed the detailed ink drawing to her proudly. "Wouldn't it be cool to be buried in a Formula 1 racing car casket?"

"No, it wouldn't!" Ana snapped. "Stop thinking like that."

Zackary admired his sketch. "Might as well go out in style."

Ana didn't want her brother to die, and this kind of talk made her angry. "It would be much better to get well and drive a *real* Formula 1 racing car."

"That's never gonna happen." Zackary sighed.

"Happy thoughts, healthy body."

"I'm a goner. Might as well face facts and plan my funeral."

"You're impossible!" Frustrated, Ana wanted to snatch the horrible sketch and crumple it up. But that would only annoy him and possibly trigger a Zack attack—which would annoy her. Plus, Zack attacks drained her brother's precious vitality. Sighing, she slipped the books into her satchel to read later.

Determined to derail her brother's obsession with his own death, she said, "Come on. Let's go check out that old Rolls Royce."

"Bentley," he corrected. "I'm not finished with my drawing."

"No, it was a Rolls Royce. I'm sure of it."

"You're wrong."

"Prove it."

"You'll see. It's a Bentley. An amateur mistake." Zackary carefully put the lid back on his pen. He closed his spiral-bound notebook, slid the pen carefully into the spiral, and put it into his small backpack. Sometimes he was so meticulous it made her want to scream.

As he packed up, she scanned the library walls and noticed some old framed family photos. One showed a much younger Uncle Shockley.

"Check this out. Uncle Shockley and Dad—eons ago."

Ana studied the family photo. It showed the two brothers, Uncle Shockley Zest and Ace Zest: the mad scientist and the movie mogul. Ace Zest's extremely pregnant second wife glowed. Uncle Shockley's ex-wife held a newborn. Several of their cousins were in the photo, as well as their older half-brother, Garrett, and half-sister, Maxwell, who were teenagers in this photo.

"You look like our mother. Even pregnant, she's petite, like an elf."

"Mmm." Zackary examined the old photo. "You look like our half-sister, Maxwell."

Ana peered at her older half-sister, Maxwell, then snorted. "Hardly. She's much prettier."

"That goes without saying, Ana Banana," teased Zackary.

"Too bad she's dead. Do you think that's why our father is so mean to me? 'Cause I remind him of his dead daughter?"

"Could be." Zackary shrugged. "But more likely, it's your annoying personality and your freaky purple eyes."

"*Violet*," Ana corrected. "Like—"

"Elizabeth Taylor," mocked Zackary, speaking in concert with his sister. "The movie star."

IN THE GARAGE, Zackary pointed out the Bentley insignia, proving his sister wrong. Ana shrugged.

But the vehicle prototype had a magnetic pull on Zackary.

"It's unlocked!" Zackary plopped himself in the driver's seat and ran his fingers over the steering wheel with delight. He threw his backpack with his sketchbook and pens into the back seat.

Ana cleverly mimicked Uncle Shockley's voice. "And don't forget, kids. The experimental car is strictly off-limits."

"Not bad. But his voice is deeper."

Ana deepened her voice to a baritone and tried again. "And don't forget, kids. The experimental car is strictly off-limits."

Zackary grinned. "Better."

Ana sat in the passenger seat and inhaled the new car smell, a faint mixture of plastic, leatherette, and ozone.

"He forgot the key." Zackary pointed to the key fob, which was still in the cup holder. It was a black plastic key in a black plastic well, so the black on black was nearly invisible. Zackary grinned and snuggled into the driver's seat. "Now I can die a happy man."

"You're hardly a man. And stop obsessing about kicking the bucket."

Zackary shrugged. "I'll stop when you stop being such a bossy big sister. Like that's ever gonna happen."

The sleek interior was like the cockpit of a modern private plane, but extra wires, cables, and knobs seemed to have been added by their uncle. "What's our mad scientist uncle up to?"

"Good question."

Ana rummaged in the center console and discovered a smartphone and a cable to plug it into the car.

"Maybe that's the brains. Some special apps or programming or something," Zackary said.

"Could be." Ana plugged in the cable, connecting the smartphone to the touchscreen mounted on the dashboard. But the smartphone was locked. "It's locked."

"Try the door code," suggested Zackary.

"Good idea!" She punched in the door code Uncle Shockley had given them before he had left for the day. "Six ... two ... three ... seven. Nope, that's not it."

"Hmmm ... our uncle is a scientist. Try pi."

"Apple or cherry?"

Zackary rolled his eyes. "Not pie, *pi!* You know, it's the number you get when ... I dunno, something to do with a circle."

"And that number is ...?"

Zackary checked his smartphone, then said, "3.14159. Try that."

"Say it again, Zee." As Zackary read the numbers aloud, Ana entered them. But it didn't work. "That's not it. Only one more try. Then we'll be locked out."

The kids hesitated.

Zackary took the phone from Ana and examined its reflective surface, twisting it this way and that and noting slight smudges in the light. He brightened. "I know! Let's try the house code ... but *backward!*"

"Are you sure? It's our last chance."

"You got a better idea, Ana Banana?"

"No. You're the tech wiz. Go for it."

Zackary entered the code. "Seven ... three ... two ... six."

The smartphone unlocked and the dashboard screen shimmered, mirroring the phone screen.

"Brilliant, Zee! How did you know?" said Ana.

"The smudges." Zackary grinned, proud of his detective work. "Fingerprints on the numbers. If the door code didn't work forward, it had to work backward."

"Clever."

Zackary and Ana took turns swiping the phone's touch screen a few times. They discovered maps, music, and farting sounds that made them giggle.

"Hey. What's this?" Zackary asked.

On screen was the Marvelous Multiverse app, something they'd never seen. It revealed a dizzying array of stars, planets, nebulae, and black holes, all connected by a vast network of shimmering lines in various colors, forming a kaleidoscope of galaxies. The intricate map suggested the multiverse—multiple galaxies slightly offset from each other.

Spellbound, Ana stared map which seemed to promise untold adventures. "The Marvelous Multiverse app … I wonder what it does?"

CHAPTER 7
THE MARVELOUS MULTIVERSE APP

"It probably picks up where Google Maps leaves off," said Zackary.

Text rolled across the screen: *Destination?*

Zackary touched the screen, which activated audio.

"My name is Leeves. I am your Marvelous Multiverse concierge," said the AI-simulated voice of a British butler. "Destination?"

"Oh, fun! It's VR. Where's the headset?" said Ana.

"Maybe the whole car is the headset?"

The kids glanced at each other, intrigued. Curiosity warred with caution.

As usual with Ana, curiosity won. "Let's try it!"

"Is this a good idea?"

"Of course not." Ana grinned mischievously. "Anything worth doing always starts as a bad idea."

Zackary hesitated. "We're going to get in trouble."

"Nothing new there. Besides, anything's better than being bored. Come on. I need your help, Zee. You know I'm hopeless with tech."

"Hopeless doesn't even begin to cover it. You're like Sir Smashum Uppe—you look at things and they break."

"That's a bit harsh," Ana protested.

"I don't think we should do this. Remember what our uncle said."

Ana made her voice a squeaky soprano. "And don't forget, kids. The experimental car is strictly off-limits."

They both laughed, breaking the tension.

The text on the screen blinked enticingly: *Destination?*

"If you do not have a specific destination in mind, may I recommend a random joyride? Once you complete the facial recognition scan, I will tailor your joyride to provide the optimal experience." His silky British accent suggested that everything was completely under control.

"Awesome!" Ana grabbed the smartphone and eagerly positioned her face for the facial recognition scan.

The Marvelous Multiverse concierge scanned her face. "What is your name?"

"Zorana Zest."

"Are you crazy? We should absolutely, positively

not monkey around with this!" Zackary's eyes were white and wild, like those of a panicked horse. He seemed on the verge of a Zack attack.

"When were electric cars invented?" Ana asked quickly.

Zackary immediately shifted from freak-out mode to lecturer mode, becoming calm. "Most people think it was Elon Musk with the Tesla, but in fact, the electric car was invented much earlier. Did you know that Ferdinand Porsche, the founder of Porsche, developed an electric car in 1898? He also created the first hybrid electric car.

"Really? What happened?"

"The Model T Ford was cheaper and became super popular."

"Come on, let's try this VR," Ana coaxed, now that Zackary was calm. "What could possibly go wrong?"

Zackary snorted. "The last time you said that—"

"That was a rhetorical question. Don't you know what *rhetorical* means?"

"Of course I do," lied Zackary. "Have you got your contacts?"

"Yes." Ana fished her contact lens case out of her satchel, which was at her feet. Her father insisted she carry them with her at all times so she could conceal her purple eyes.

"Puffer?"

"Got it. OCD much?" Ana asked, referring to her brother's obsessive-compulsive behavior.

"Don't start, purple eyes."

"*Violet*. Like Elizabeth Taylor."

"The movie star," the kids chorused together, but Zackary's tone was mocking.

"I don't think Dad makes you wear colored contacts to keep the paparazzi away."

"You can't be sure about that. I was incredible in that Hallmark movie."

"You didn't have any lines."

"I did so—they just ended up on the cutting room floor. And I got great reviews for my performance in *Peter Pan*!"

"In the *school* newspaper. How can a girl play Peter Pan? That's wrong."

"That just shows how little you know about live theater. Peter Pan is always played by a girl."

"I don't care about theater. That's your shtick."

"Ready to go?" Leeves inquired.

"What do you say, Zackary? Shall we give it a whirl? Remember when we went to Universal Studios? It might be awesome like that."

"I rather doubt it," said Zackary gloomily.

"You never know until you try. You're in the driver's seat. It's up to you, Captain Zee."

Zackary sat up straighter, like a captain in a starship, and commanded, "Make it so, Number One."

A thrill of delight tingled through Ana. She loved pushing the envelope and distained the mundane.

"Leeves, set destination to Random Joyride. Tailored to my facial recognition scan," said Ana eagerly.

"As you wish, Miss Zorana Zest," said Leeves.

Unexpectedly, a silver film covered the car's windows.

"Wicked," said Zackary, impressed.

"Please fasten your seatbelts," said Leeves.

The kids clicked in.

The computer counted down. "Ready in five ... four ... three ... two ... one!"

Suddenly, they were spinning, whirling in a stomach-roiling vortex, like being on a roller coaster. Inside the PUP, warning alarms blared. The world swirled with all the colors of the rainbow, then became white.

CHAPTER 8
CRASH LANDING

VERDANT, TELLUSORA.

The Parallel Universe Pod exploded from the vortex of the space-time continuum and crashed. The silver film covering the windshield retracted, giving the kids a stomach-churning view as it scraped by one tree, narrowly missed another, and tore a huge hunk out of a third tree. Branches squealed against the chassis.

The PUP plowed into a massive tree trunk and abruptly stopped, jerking Zackary and Ana forward. Their seatbelts kept them from being launched out through the windshield. The high-pitched squealing sound ceased.

"You OK?" Ana asked her brother.

"As banged up as this car." Zackary rubbed his bruised shin.

"Where are we?"

"How on Earth should I know?"

Ana tapped the computer screen. "Leeves? Where are we?"

"The outskirts of the city of Prosperus in Verdant. This world is called Tellusora by the inhabitants, Lokey by some others." Every word came out more slowly than the one before as the battery died. "Regrettably, due to a slight miscalculation of scale, we are now out of hydrogen. Please refuel."

The fuel gauge read *E* for empty.

"Out of fuel? That's great. Just great," Zackary said, snorting in irritation. "Leeves, where's the nearest hydrogen refueling station?"

"Unknown," Leeves answered. "Have fun on your adventure. I do humbly apologize, but I must leave you now." The computer screen faded, and the voice of Leeves died.

"Just when I was starting to like him. Come on," said Ana.

Zackary and Ana tumbled out of the PUP to inspect the damage. The pine tree's trunk was chewed up, and the front bumper of the car was crumpled.

Ana smelled the invigorating scent of pine as she examined the damaged bumper. She slid her hand against the once-perfectly smooth chassis, which was now warm and dented. The car was not a hologram.

"This is real. We're not in a VR simulation."

"Look at our uncle's car." Zackary mourned the loss of the car's sleek perfection. "Dad'll kill you."

"Kill *me*? Kill *us*, you mean. Why do I always get blamed?"

"Because it's always your fault. Look at the destruction!" Zackary pointed to the trail of broken tree branches in their wake. "You're a disaster magnet!"

"*I'm* a disaster magnet? *You're* a disaster magnet!"

"Takes one to know one!" Zackary snapped, his eyes white and wild, on the brink of a Zack attack.

Ana took a breath to calm herself. "Okay, you're right already. We are a pair of disaster magnets. What is the range of a Mirai?"

Zack shifted into lecture mode, becoming calm. "It has a range of three hundred miles or five hundred kilometers on a full tank. Most people don't know that refueling with hydrogen takes a few minutes, and that's a fraction of the time to recharge an electric car. And it can go from zero to sixty miles per hour in nine seconds."

"What story shall we tell people?" Ana asked, disinterested in cars but interested in staying out of trouble, which meant performing a convincing new character. And every character needs a backstory.

"Huh? What are you talking about?"

"We can't go around telling everyone the truth. That's asking for trouble. We don't want complete strangers to know that we took our uncle's car without permission."

"'Oh, what a tangled web we weave, when first we practice to deceive.' Who said that?" Zackary asked.

"Shakespeare, I think."

"Wrong!" Zackary said gleefully. "It was Sir Walter Scott."

"You memorized that just to trip me up, didn't you?"

"Of course."

"Listen, we're not *lying*. We're simply not telling people things that are none of their business. We're *acting*. Big difference. Actors are great. Fame and fortune and all that. Think of it as improv," said Ana.

"You're never a straight shooter—you're always bendy, like a banana, Ana Banana."

"Straight is boring. Besides, I gotta live up to my nickname. As Dad always says, 'There's no business—'"

"'—like show business,'" Zackary chimed in, and the kids finished the oft-quoted sentence together.

"How are we going to remember where we left the PUP?" Zackary fiddled with his phone, frustrated. "I can't drop a pin. Does your compass work?"

"Every direction is north." Ana played with various buttons on her smartphone. The flashlight turned on. "The flashlight works!"

"Great. That's super useful in broad daylight."

Ana shook her phone—because that always works. She took a selfie.

"A selfie won't help. Get some landmarks in the photo. I'll sketch a quick map." Zackary took out his spiral sketchbook and black pen. He surveyed the surroundings and spotted an ominous castle in the distance. "Wicked castle!"

"Could that be Hampton Court Palace?"

"How should I know? Check Google."

Ana tried, but her phone failed to bring up an image of Hampton Court Palace. "No signal."

Zackary sketched the landmarks. The distant mountain range had a distinctive black tusk peak. Nearby, a two-lane dirt road was marred with tire tracks from the PUP's crash landing. In a nearby pasture, a few horses regarded the intruders with alert suspicion. Next to this rolling pasture were farmers' fields.

Meanwhile, Ana wandered around the PUP to get the castle in the backdrop. She snapped a few photos.

Ana heard a whimper and hurried toward the sound. The PUP had scraped by an oak tree, tearing a massive tree branch away from the trunk. This leafy cage had trapped a little dog. It whined, pleading for help. One leg was pinned at an unnatural angle.

"Easy now. Easy. I'll get you out of there." Ana tugged the heavy branches away. She shouted, "I found a dog!"

Zackary glanced up from sketching the map and muttered, "My sister, the animal magnet." He called out, "Dogs bite. Don't get rabies!"

Zackary wandered around the experimental car, continuing to sketch landmarks.

The lapdog had long white and caramel-colored hair fringing its cute but forlorn face. Its brown oval eyes melted Ana's heart. One hind leg hung limp and useless.

"There, there." Humming to soothe her nerves, Ana gently lifted the injured dog and it yelped in pain. But instead of biting her, the dog wagged the feathery white tail that curled over its back, tickling her skin. It looked like a Lhasa apso with a bit of a miniature schnauzer.

"Who's a good boy?" Ana crooned.

The dog barked, and it sounded like *I am! I am!*

Ana blinked in surprise.

Then the dog whined in pain, which needed no translation.

"We have to get this dog to the vet," she called, cuddling the warm animal.

"Leave the dog," Zackary said, his voice cracking. "The dog is the least of our problems."

"I think his leg is broken. We can't leave him here." Still carrying the lapdog, Ana joined her brother by the PUP and saw that all the color had drained from his face.

"This is bad. Terrible." Zackary pointed to something peeking out from underneath the PUP. "We ran over someone."

"Oh, no!" Ana gasped.

They had crushed someone underneath their car. They saw a young woman's well-manicured hand peeking out of a green sleeve. Both kids stared at the hand, horrified.

"Hello? Are you okay?" Ana asked. "Hello?"

No answer.

"*Okay?* Are you crazy? She's *dead*." Zackary's face was ashen.

"Why do you always jump to the worst possible conclusion?" said Ana.

"Why are you always so absurdly optimistic?"

"Check her pulse," said Ana.

"No way!" Zackary took a step back, horrified.

"Fine, I'll do it. Hold the dog." Ana thrust the dog into Zackary's arms.

Neither the dog nor Zackary seemed happy about that. Zackary put the dog down, and the lapdog yelped in pain.

A curious crow on a nearby tree eyed them with a glassy eye.

"We need to get help." Ana kneeled beside the PUP.

"She's beyond help."

"You don't know that." Ana checked the woman's

wrist for a pulse. Not finding one, her mind whirled with dread. "No pulse."

"Told you so. She's dead. We killed her," Zackary said miserably.

"It was an accident!"

"Accident or no accident, we're murderers." Zackary's voice trembled. "We're in trouble now."

Ana gasped as the woman's hand transformed. They both watched, horrified, as the hand rapidly aged, changing from the color of cream to become spotted with age, then gnarled. Finally, the hand, arm, and figure completely disintegrated, leaving behind only an empty green velvet dress.

With a tinkle, the golden cuff that had been on her wrist fell onto a rock. There was another tinkle as a second golden cuff rolled into view. Tentatively, Ana reached out and collected the two heavy bracelets. Entranced, she slid the golden cuffs onto her wrists. As if they had a will of their own, the bracelets snapped shut.

From the nearby tree, the crow flew away.

"Stop monkeying about with jewelry. Let's get out of here," insisted Zackary.

"We can't leave the scene of a hit-and-run." Ana's mind was reeling, but she knew that leaving was wrong.

"It's too late to help that lady. If we stay, we're in danger. But she'll still be dead. Or vanished—or whatever she is. We're not in England anymore." Zackary tugged his sister toward their experimental car, forgetting momentarily that it was out of fuel. He desperately wanted to escape. "Come on!"

The dog whined.

"We've got to get help for this little fella." Ana scooped up the dog, and it wagged its tail, happy to be back in her arms.

"Are you *insane?*" Zackary tried to reason with his sister. "This is serious! We need a lawyer, not a vet."

But before they could leave—or get help—a tall, grim figure suddenly grabbed the kids. Their feet left the ground as they were hoisted up. Her heart racing, Ana stared into the strange, inhuman face of her captor.

Ana and Zackary screamed.

CHAPTER 9
MURDERERS!

Holding Zackary and Ana suspended by their collars like two wayward puppies, their diabolical captor interrogated them with a stream of incomprehensible words. He jerked his chin toward the now-vacant green dress pinned under the wheel.

"It's not our fault," Zackary protested. "We didn't mean to land on her."

Still holding them suspended, he took long strides toward the ominous castle. His hair was an oily black, sticking to his high forehead in limp strands. He resembled an ugly, scarred human with a strangely rectangular head. Their abductor gave them a tongue-lashing in his strange language, but the kids couldn't understand a word.

Ana's hands trembled, and she barely managed to

squeak out the words, "Who are you? Where are you taking us?" Guilt washed over her for accidentally killing the woman in the green dress. Ana's eyes darted around helplessly.

Nearing the castle, their jailer held them aloft as he stomped past the row of cypress trees and a stone wall with an ornate iron gate that stood open. A cobbled driveway led to a roundabout for cars—or, more likely, carriages—that brought visitors to the palatial front entrance. But their captor ducked around the side of the building, stomped past a vegetable-and-herb garden, and knocked at a modest back door with his boot.

After a moment, Cook opened the door, wiping one hand on her flour-dusty apron. Her other hand held a huge, sharp knife. Her eyes widened at the sight of two kids held captive.

They had never seen anyone like her. (Later, they learned she was a Feinmuncher, a species famous for their culinary magic, and everyone called her Cook.) As round as an apple and as short as a dwarf, her stupendous feet were bare. Her toenails were painted a gaudy shade of pink, but no shade of pink could ever make those huge hairy toes appear feminine.

Their abductor said something to her in their strange language. She waved them in. Enticing scents of freshly baked bread, garlic, and rosemary enveloped them. He set the disoriented kids firmly down on their feet. His body language clearly indicated, *Don't move—or there will be trouble.* He shut and locked the kitchen door.

Frozen with fear, Ana surveyed the expansive kitchen. Shiny copper pots hung from the ceiling. Sliced potatoes, carrots, celery, and onions stood on the countertop beside a bowl. Stools flanked the counter, creating a place to eat. A pantry door stood ajar, revealing enough china and crystal to serve an elegant dinner to dozens of guests.

Their abductor slipped into the pantry and retrieved a tiny vial from the top shelf. He was exceptionally tall and the pant legs were too short in his ill-fitting suit.

Cook waved her huge chef's knife at them, her threat loud and clear.

Ana clutched the whimpering lapdog like a shield. She still wore the two mysterious cuffs on her wrists. Zackary's face was as pale as a peeled potato.

As if he were about to perform a magic trick, their captor showed off tiny orange eels swimming in the slender glass vial. He plucked out a wriggling eel and popped it into Zackary's ear with lightning speed.

"Hey!" Zackary protested. "What're you doing?"

Then their captor popped another squirming eel into Ana's ear.

"Babbler-eel," he explained, his words now understandable despite his lisp. "Univerthal tranthlator. Can you underthtand me now?"

The kids nodded. Ana rubbed her ear, which tickled. (It felt like having a bit of water in your ear after swimming.)

"I'm Egor, and thith here ith Cook. They killed the Emerald Centhor." Egor pointed a calloused hand at them accusingly with long, chipped fingernails. (Later, they discovered he was a Gleb, a species known for their quirky intelligence, unquestioning loyalty, and surgical ability.)

Cook's mouth opened in a wide O of surprise, and she recoiled. "Oh my word! The Emerald Censor is dead? These kids killed her?"

"In a word, yeth. They are murdererth."

The kids glanced at each other, terrified. They had never been in more trouble. And that was saying something.

CHAPTER 10
THE CRUEL QUEEN

CROWNED CITADEL, REXHAVEN, AVENIR.

Far away, under the domed royal biosphere in a sophisticated, high-tech room, Queen Crimson reclined on a dark-green leatherette couch. A diamond tiara sparkled in her red hair, and she was snuggled in a red royal robe edged with ermine. Under the robe, she wore a black cashmere turtleneck, pants, and knee-high boots.

The windowless room was dimly lit. Several enormous TV screens glowed. One displayed a fire flickering in a hearth. Another flat screen showed an alien blue fish swimming in a fish tank. A third revealed a twinkling pinwheel galaxy with a swirl of planets and stars.

"Opus Die refuses to give me another mining

permit! I'll never restore Avenir to her former glory without more oxygen. A *lot* more oxygen," Queen Crimson complained in her husky voice.

"Is that true, my queen?" asked a silky voice in a deferential tone.

"Of course it's true! Have you looked outside?"

"Of course not, my queen. My model does not perambulate." The AI therapist had a kind face and attractive torso—but no legs. Instead, N2ME-C was hard-wired into a blinking computer and artificial intelligence triggered her questions.

"Well, it's a barren wasteland. Only the dome protects this measly corner of Avenir from ruin. It's completely unacceptable. I *must* get those mining permits! Or we're condemned to wither and die. Rexhaven will be obliterated. Avenir will be toxic. We won't even be able to maintain the atmosphere here in the Crowned Citadel unless we get more pure air. Worse yet—what's the point of being the queen of a barren wasteland?"

"I hear that it's important to you to be queen of a thriving land."

"I was born to *rule*—not to be Opus Die's tool in another world."

"How is it going? Being a Censor on Lokey?" N2ME-C asked mildly.

"The natives call it Tellusora. But Lokey is a better

fit, as it is low key and low tech. I have no idea what Opus Die sees in that backward place. Horses and carriages! No robots, no hot running water, no electricity, not even any AI therapists. I can't stand it. I absolutely must revive Avenir to her previous splendor. I *will* get those oxygen mining permits."

"Do you think Opus Die will grant them?"

"Opus Die doesn't care about Avenir. He has no vision. He can't see the potential. But he absolutely *must* increase my quota."

"And if he refuses?"

"I'll think of something. But I'd prefer to persuade him."

"How do you intend to persuade him?" N2ME-C asked.

"I'll make my move at the gala at his palace next week. He's more likely to succumb to my charms in person."

"Will you take Prince Hunter with you to the gala?"

The queen released a bitter huff of laughter. "He wouldn't be safe amongst all those sharks. Besides, all he wants to do is stay here and play video games. It'll rot his brain. He needs to get out, go places, learn things! Why, when I was his age, I was doing things. Top of my class at the Assassin's Academy—"

Suddenly, the door slammed open, interrupting Queen Crimson mid-sentence. Prince Hunter barged in, excited. He was a handsome teenager with ivory skin and a luxurious mane of dark hair. "Mom!"

Queen Crimson sat up, her face dark with rage. "I told you never to interrupt my therapy sessions! Can't you see the red light is on? She pointed towards the bright red light next to the door.

"But you told me to tell you immediately, no matter what. The Emerald Censor's light has gone out."

"What?" Queen Crimson peered at her cuffs, which were adorned with runes and rubies. One engraved star featured five different-colored gems at the tips of each point. Four of the five jewels glowed, but the green one did not. "The emerald has gone out. Impossible."

"Could it be a faulty reading?" Prince Hunter asked.

"Unlikely," said Queen Crimson.

"What else is possible?" asked the AI therapist.

"She's dead."

"Was she murdered?" Prince Hunter asked, licking his full lips and relishing the thought.

"If it was murder, there'll be hell to pay! I will find the murderers and destroy them. The people of Tellusora must not get ideas into their fool heads about killing Censors," said Queen Crimson.

"Could the Emerald Censor have died of natural

causes?" the AI therapist asked in her usual neutral manner.

"There was nothing natural about the Emerald Censor, so I doubt it. I have to go to Tellusora and get to the bottom of this."

"Why not monitor Lokey from here?" asked Prince Hunter.

"You can do that. Monitor the readouts from the raven sims. Track the last known whereabouts of the Emerald Censor. See how she was killed. If I catch the murderer and eliminate the threat, Opus Die will owe me one. Then he will have to give me those mining permits."

"And if he doesn't?"

"I will not be denied," said Queen Crimson, her voice like a rusty blade. She started packing a suitcase with essential items, including a series of high-tech plastic gadgets. "I hate going back in time. I hate that stupid magnetic portal force-field. I can't take this ... or this ... or this!" Annoyed, Crimson removed her tiara, her blaster, and a bejeweled knife she had concealed in her boots.

"I don't know why you're packing. There's no one here but us. Are you expecting a robot revolt?"

"At the Assassin's Academy, I was trained to always be prepared. It's when you think you're safe that you're in the most danger. Never be complacent. Always be vigilant. A lesson you ignore."

"Nothing ever happens here. It's the dullest place in the multiverse, more like a wasteland than a kingdom."

"Avenir used to be thriving. You should have seen it! There were lively parties on the rooftops of skyscrapers with dancing and all kinds of music. Rexhaven was a hive of technological innovation and creativity. And it will be again, I swear."

"So you keep saying."

Queen Crimson glared at her son. "Don't sass your queen. And don't stay up all night playing video games."

"I'm *making* video games, Mother. I'm a video game *designer*. Why can't you respect that?"

"That's no career for a prince. Enroll in the Assassin's Academy. It was good enough for me. It's good enough for you. If I hadn't been on Tellusora learning how to run people through with a sword, I would have been fried to a crisp like everyone else on Avenir. Then you never would have been born."

"But I don't want to become an assassin. I want to be a video game designer. I *am* a video game designer."

"Why kill people in a game when you can kill them for real?" Queen Crimson licked her scarlet lips.

"People all over the multiverse buy my games. You should see my cryptocurrency account!"

Queen Crimson scoffed. "What use is cryptocurrency when your kingdom needs *oxygen*? How long can you survive without cryptocurrency? A long time. How long can you survive without air? Only a few minutes!"

"She's got a point, son," said the AI therapist.

"That's *Prince Hunter* to you." Prince Hunter grabbed the remote control from where it lay on an end table near his mother.

"Right. I formally apologize, Prince Hunter," said the AI therapist.

"That's enough out of you," said Prince Hunter.

He clicked the remote and turned off the AI therapist. She whirred and then became silent and still.

"Why don't I ever get to do what *I* want?" Prince Hunter demanded.

"You're the crown prince. Royalty has its privileges—and its responsibilities. End of discussion. Enroll in the Assassin's Academy. The deadline is tonight."

"Are the classes at night?"

"They were in my day. But don't worry. We've pretty much perfected the sunscreen."

"Pretty much? Why should I risk my hide to go to a stupid school? I'd rather stay here."

"You're a prince. You can't stay on Avenir your whole life."

"I don't see why not." Prince Hunter sulked.

"It's time for the next chapter of your life. But I don't have time for this discussion right now." Queen Crimson finished packing and snapped her suitcase shut. "I'm off." She strode to the door and gave her son a quick goodbye hug, which he tolerated.

"Bring back some fresh meat," Prince Hunter said.

"You can eat frozen," said Queen Crimson.

"Fresh is better." Prince Hunter licked his sensuous lips. "I like it when they run."

CHAPTER 11
HEROES

LORD ORATOR'S CASTLE, VERDANT, TELLUSORA.

In the kitchen with Cook, Egor, and Zackary, Ana took a deep breath. "It's all my fault," she confessed. "My brother is innocent. But it was an accident. Honestly!"

Egor and Cook ignored her confession, but Zackary gazed at her with gratitude. The little dog whined in Ana's arms.

"How do you know it was the Emerald Censor?" Cook asked Egor.

Egor pointed to the two golden cuffs on Ana's wrists. Tiny emeralds and complex runes adorned the bracelets.

"Her cuffth," lisped Egor.

"Is she really dead, Egor?" Cook asked anxiously. "Really, truly dead?"

"Really, truly dead," Egor confirmed. "No one could get these cuffth off her if thhe wath alive."

"And the body?" asked Cook.

"Flattened by their horthleth carriage. The body turned to dutht and dithappeared."

Cook's face lit up with joy. She clapped her hands with delight. "Hurrah! Hurrah! The evil Emerald Censor is dead!"

"We have theen the latht of her."

Short, rotund Cook and tall, lanky Egor linked arms and danced around the kitchen with glee. They made an improbable couple, but their delight was contagious.

Color seeped back into Zackary's ashen face. Ana exhaled a shaky breath.

Cook spun around the kitchen dance floor with Egor. "My prayers have been answered! We've been delivered from her wrath. I had no idea how we were going to escape the Emerald Censor."

Egor's face cracked into a gruesome smile, revealing crooked yellow teeth. "A thtrange vehicle cruthing her wath not in my top ten."

"It's the Prophecy come true!" said Cook.

"Hurrah, hurrah!" Egor gave a lopsided grin. He let go of his rotund dance partner reluctantly. Did he have a thing for Cook?

Cook smoothed her apron, flushed. "You need to find yourself a Gleborina, Egor."

Egor sighed wistfully. "If only I had another heart, perhaps thome Gleborina would find me worthy."

"What's wrong with your heart?" Cook asked.

"It's too thmall for true love," Egor admitted sorrowfully.

"If you want another heart, go see the Wizard Snapdragon," Cook said.

Egor perked up. "You think the Wizard Thnapdragon would help me?"

"Why not? She's a powerful wizard and can do anything. I've heard tell that she's willing to help those with a worthy cause."

At the mention of the Wizard Snapdragon, the dog in Ana's arms stopped whining and cocked his head with interest. The dog's head bounced back and forth as if he were watching a tennis match as he followed their conversation.

"Are we in trouble?" Ana asked in a tremulous voice.

"Trouble? Trouble! Not with us, dearies. You are heroes!" Cook declared.

Ana and Zackary exchanged a giddy glance as going from villains to heroes in a flash gave their hearts whiplash.

"Will they charge us with murder?" Zackary asked, his voice cracking.

"Not if we can help it," said Cook. "But Opus Die must not get wind of this. Or you two won't be the only ones who hang." She diced vegetables with a vengeance. "Lord Orator will be pleased that you eliminated the Emerald Censor."

"Sensor—like, she senses things?" Zackary asked.

"No. Like *chop-chop*." Egor made a cleaving motion with his hands. "She eliminateth thingth."

"She eliminates things? Oh—you mean she *censors* things," Zackary said.

"That'th what I thaid."

"We've got to get rid of the evidence. Or another wicked Censor will come knocking. And we'll be in no end of trouble. *Again.*"

"Leave it to me." Egor strode purposefully toward the door.

The dog barked, "Help me! My leg hurts!"

Ana gazed at Zackary. "Did you hear that?"

"The dog barked. So what?"

"He said, 'Help me, my leg hurts.' Didn't you hear it?"

Zackary frowned. "Any idiot can see the dog's leg is broken. You don't have to pretend the dog talks."

Ana furrowed her brows, annoyed at her disbelieving brother.

Cook swooped in. "Dearie me, let's have a look at that."

"I think his leg is broken," Ana apologized.

Cook's face softened as she gazed affectionately at the small dog. "Wait, Egor! My thoughts were bubbling like a pot of overheated soup, but I should have noticed earlier. Take our Veto and see what you can do. Poor thing's in pain."

"Finally!" barked Veto. "About time you paid attention to me."

"Surely you heard that, Zee," Ana insisted.

Zackary huffed. "It barked. So what Ana Banana?"

"The dog said, 'Finally! About time you paid attention to me.'"

"Fibber," Zackary accused, rolling his eyes.

"Am not!" Ana glared at her brother, who shrugged. "Just because you can't understand dog doesn't mean I can't."

CHAPTER 12
ANIMAL WHISPERER

Egor tried to take the dog from Ana, but Veto growled and nipped him, unwilling to leave the sanctuary of Ana's arms.

"Are you okay?" Ana asked Egor.

"A little love bite. Ith nothing." Egor shrugged it off, then admitted shyly to Zackary, "Though I'd prefer a love bite from a Gleborina."

Zackary's eyebrows rose in surprise.

Veto whined as he struggled to remain in Ana's arms. He snarled and nipped Egor again, refusing to be handed off to him.

"Rest easy, Veto. Egor will stitch you up, and no mistake," said Cook, but her words didn't soothe the whining dog.

"He smells awful. Icky chemical stink. I don't trust him," snarled Veto in disgust.

"Did you hear that?" Ana asked, turning to Cook.

"Of course we did, dearie. He's yapping away."

"He said he doesn't trust you," Ana told Egor.

"I can thee that," said Egor.

"But didn't you hear him *say* that?"

"My hearing ith not what it uthed to be," Egor said diplomatically.

"Fibbermeister," Zackary shot accusingly at his sister.

Ana fixed a withering gaze on her brother, then returned to caring for the hurt dog.

"Easy, now, easy." Ana rocked Veto and hummed "Ana's Song," the lullaby that always soothed her.

As if enchanted, Veto calmed down. He licked Ana's face, wagged his tail, and then placidly allowed Egor to take him.

Observing this, Cook muttered, "Animal whisperer."

"I'll fix him up," promised Egor.

With her hands on her stout hips, Cook warned, "Don't get creative! Lord Orator will want Veto back, not some circus experiment."

Egor grunted and left with Veto in his arms.

"Will Veto be okay?" Ana fretted.

"Trust in our surgical maestro. He'll mend Veto's leg like an artist, skillfully weaving stitches as surely as I can truss a turkey to keep all the delectable stuffing inside. Glebs are stirring at that sort of thing," Cook said. "The only thing they can't operate on is their own hearts."

"Why would anyone want to operate on their own heart?" Ana asked.

"Because it's broken, of course. Glebs can be unstable when brokenhearted. Behind every great Gleb is a Gleborina. But he'd need a powerful wizard like the Wizard Snapdragon to fix his broken heart."

"The Wizard Snapdragon can fix a broken heart?" Zackary asked, incredulous.

"Can I bake bread?" said Cook.

"Can she cure a sick person?" Zackary's voice wavered.

"She can heal anyone of anything, or so I've heard. She cannot bring people back from the dead. But that wouldn't be natural."

Ana and Zackary exchanged a meaningful glance.

"Where can we find the Wizard Snapdragon?" Ana asked, her voice cracking. "My brother's not one-hundred percent."

"I'm a goner," Zackary said. "They *say* I'm in remission ... but I *know* it's just a matter of time before the Grim Reaper comes for me."

Cook raised her eyebrows in surprise. Zackary appeared frail—the pale skin, the wispy blonde hair, the thin body.

"He's immune-o-compromised," Ana said, stumbling over the long word. "The chemo and radiation made him vulnerable to disease."

Cook's brow furrowed in confusion.

"But I've designed a really cool Formula 1 racing car casket. Do you want to see it?" Zackary grabbed his sketchbook, flipped through to find the right page, then showed his elaborate drawing to Cook.

"Er ... ah ... very stirring," said Cook, floundering for the right words.

"How can we find this Wizard Snapdragon?"

"If only Lord Orator were here, he'd know. But we can ask my cousin Rosalind at Bluebells Inn. What, with all the travelers coming and going, she might know." Cook pointed to the stools flanking the countertop. "In the meantime, sit, eat, and tell me your story."

The kids settled on the stools. Cook put on the kettle and set plates and bowls on the countertop in front of them.

Scrutinizing Ana's face for the first time, Cook noticed her striking violet eyes. "Your eyes. They're so *purple!*"

"They're *violet*—like Elizabeth Taylor." Ana corrected automatically.

Zackary rolled his eyes.

"Is that your mother?" Cook asked.

Zackary sniggered.

"No, no, she's an old-time movie star." Ana shot a dark look at her brother.

"What's a movie star?" said Cook.

"Uh …" Ana realized her mistake. Tellusora didn't have movies—or movie stars.

Zackary chimed in. "It's part of her religion."

"Oh … religion, I see," Cook said, seeing nothing of the sort but veering away from that dangerous topic to safer ground. "Anyway, everybody's got a story, and I want to hear yours. Your story is the most important thing you have. It's the most precious thing you can give away—and still keep. It's like sharing a recipe, but a recipe for life."

Ana yearned to discover her own story. Her heart ached and her chest felt hollow. If she had known a mother's love, perhaps things would be different. Perhaps she'd truly belong somewhere.

Cook bustled about, making a generous snack. She muttered under her breath, "Purple eyes, white hair, right age, weird ways …" She poured three cups of tea.

While Cook prepared food, Zackary sketched the intricate details on the bracelets. Ana traced a fingertip over a rune. "I wonder what these mean?"

Zackary shrugged. "They probably curse any thief who steals them."

Ana furrowed her brows. "Trust you to find a negative spin. What if they grant incredible power?"

Happy that the Emerald Censor was dead, Cook hummed as she served delicious stew, cheese, jam, butter, and freshly baked scones. A true Feinmuncher, Cook showed her gratitude through her art form: food.

"So, on with it. Who are you? Where did you come from?" asked Cook.

His mouth full, Zackary said indistinctly, "California. Well, now UK."

Ana glared at Zackary and kicked his foot under the stool.

"Cal ... If-Ornia ... Well-Now ... UK?" Cook attempted the unfamiliar words. "Never heard of it."

"I'm Zorana," Ana said.

Her brother's eyebrows shot up in surprise. Perhaps she didn't want "Ana" to be blamed for the trouble they were in.

"And I'm Zackary. There isn't much to tell. We went for a joyride—"

"He's not to blame," interrupted Ana. "We crashed. Our ... vehicle ... landed on that lady in the green dress."

"A blessed miracle!" Cook said.

Intrigued, Zackary paused with his spoon halfway to his mouth, about to ask a question, but Ana spoke first.

"It was an accident. I would never kill anyone on purpose. Neither of us would," Ana insisted.

"You might be surprised what you would do if push came to shove," Cook muttered darkly. "Especially with those purple eyes marking you as the one foretold by the Prophecy."

CHAPTER 13
DEATH BY PROPHECY

"Why're you so happy that Emerald lady is dead?" Zackary asked.

"That was no lady. That was the Emerald Censor. Dark times, I tell you. It's gotten worse and worse. Opus Die controls everything we say and do. He controls us through the four Censors—three now—and the Koercer troops."

"What's a Koercer?" Zackary asked.

"They're people turned into puppet slaves, cursed to obey every whim of the Censors," Cook said grimly. "They possess as much free will as a wooden salad bowl—and about as much fellow feeling. When a Censor commands them, they move like clockwork toys. At least you can usually hear them coming as they clatter like spoons in a drawer."

"How dreadful. Is there a cure?" asked Ana.

"None that I know of. The Koercers are like Opus Die's thought police. It's not safe to think a contrarian thought. The Muzzled Many barely seem to notice as Opus Die strips away freedoms, one by one. They don't fight back. They are like frogs in a pot. If you heat the water slowly, they don't jump out. They're cooked. *Cuisses de grenouilles*—a fine delicacy served with butter, garlic, fresh parsley, a splash of wine." Cook smacked her lips appreciatively.

"The Muzzled Many?" Ana prompted, eager to forestall a cooking lesson.

Cook sliced apples and put them into pastry shells for apple pies. "The Muzzled Many are those who don't—or can't—speak freely. Unlike the Free Few: we who refuse to be silenced." She lowered her voice to a conspiratorial whisper. "Question things that seem to be too good to be true. We're told, 'Opus Die protects you.' Is that true? What if the truth is the opposite?"

"The opposite? You mean like ... Opus Die *uses* you?" Ana asked.

"Exactly." Cook chopped apples in ferocious agreement.

"Who is Opus Die?" Zackary asked.

"He's lord and ruler of all. Controls everything. His master plan is to keep us 'tragically flawed mortals' from making mistakes—from missing the mark and sinning. Sounds good until you realize that means he's deciding everything for everyone. There's no free will, see? How do people learn except by making mistakes? Who knows whether something is a mistake? He'd certainly think killing the Emerald Censor was wrong—but I say it's right. A blessed miracle."

"Opus Die sounds evil," said Zackary.

"He is evil. But you didn't hear it from me. It's not safe to have such opinions. Not even here. Lord Orator is usually impeccably discreet, but Koercers are everywhere! You can't trust anyone. The Emerald Censor was coming to cancel him, no doubt about it. All of Lord Orator's lands, holdings, and wealth would have been seized. It would've ruined everyone connected in any way to Lord Orator. We would all have suffered—tossed out of our jobs, our homes. No one else would ever risk employing us. Our lives, our futures—canceled." Cook snorted.

Zackary and Ana finished the delicious stew, and Cook ladled more into their empty bowls. "But you saved us from all that."

"Thanks, but I'm stuffed." Pushing aside his bowl, Zackary began to sketch the cuffs with mysterious runes that Ana was wearing.

"You mentioned a prophecy. Can you tell us about it?" asked Ana.

Cook's voice took on a rich timbre as she recited the Prophecy:

*"Invaders will come from a land of
   twin sun,
Our only hope is the Chosen One.*

*Snowy hair, silver tongue, eyes lavender
   jewels,
He'll free us all from oppressive rules.*

*Born when the moon sets, rises, and is sky
   high.
Unbeaten below unblinking eye,*

*Masterverse, portal key, otherworldly
   knight,
He will break the ruthless tyrant's might."*

Intrigued, Ana leaned forward.

Cook sniffed and continued in a flat voice, "Opus Die ordered the slaughter of every child who might fulfill the Prophecy. Our three moons were scattered in the sky, one setting, one rising, and the third at its zenith—the sign of the Chosen One's birth. That was during the Year of the Iguana."

Cook glanced at Zorana. "Masterverses have white hair and purple eyes like you, Zorana. Blonde hair and light eyes marked one for the Great Culling. Even brown-haired babies with brown eyes were slaughtered. That's why there's practically no one left alive who is your age. No respect for the sanctity of life."

Cook angrily pressed pastry lids onto the tops of the apple pies. "I was head cook at Bluebells Inn at that time. The Bergers' firstborn son was born at the wrong time, the wrong year. I loved that little four-year-old boy! You should have seen him. He was so cute I wanted to eat him up! He had blonde hair and blue eyes. One day, I was making the boy's favorite cookies, biscotti, when the Koercers knocked at the door—"

BANG! BANG! Cook banged the counter with the butt of her knife to emphasize her point. Ana and Zackary jumped, startled.

"I opened the door. Unfortunately. But what choice did I have? They seized the little boy. Berndt tried to cling to my apron. He was terrified. He wailed for me to help him. I pleaded and said his eyes were *blue*—not lavender. Blue! But those mindless brutes wouldn't listen. They tore him away from my arms." Cook sniffed and wiped a tear away with a massive arm. She added mournfully, "They wouldn't even let him take a cookie."

"That's dreadful," Ana said.

"He would've been about your age now." Cook took a large hankie from her apron pocket and wiped her red eyes. Then she blew her nose with a loud trumpeting sound, which was most unladylike.

"Was he ever seen again?" Zackary asked.

"Never. They murdered that little boy. In cold blood! And for what? Power! Control! Our Berndt was not the only one. Hundreds of children were 'disappeared'—never to be seen again. But that didn't make it any easier. Our Berndt was gone, and I couldn't bear to look his parents in the face. So I came to work for Lord Orator." Cook's grief gave way to anger. "Those Koercers are like spoiled meat in the pantry, ruining everything. I *won't* let another child go missing. Not on my watch."

Cook rummaged in the pantry, took down a big cookie jar, and fished out a tiny pouch. She gave it to Ana. "Anyway, you saved us all a lot of grief by eliminating the Emerald Censor. Thank you for saving me tears."

"You don't need to—" Ana said.

Cook bristled. "Are you refusing my Tear Gift?"

"No, no, of course not. Thank you." Ana opened the iridescent pouch. Dozens of sparkling diamonds clattered onto the counter.

"Diamonds?" Zackary's eyes widened. He picked up a glittering gem. "Are these real? Genuine diamonds?"

"Of course. A Tear Gift is always diamonds," Cook said, offended.

"Wow—that's so—so generous," Ana said.

"Don't make such a fuss." Cook cleared their dishes. "You can't eat 'em. It's only diamonds."

"*Only* diamonds? They're worth a fortune!" Zackary picked up a few of the glittering gems.

"Back home, maybe. But not here, apparently," said Ana.

KNOCK! KNOCK!

Everyone jumped. Cook dropped a crockery bowl, which shattered on the floor. Zackary and Ana swept the scattered diamonds into their pockets. Who was knocking at the door?

The rapid-fire knock repeated insistently, like a woodpecker. *KNOCK! KNOCK! KNOCK!*

Was it the Koercers? Were they going to be arrested?

Cook went cautiously to the door, taking her sharp chef's knife with her.

CHAPTER 14
THE GOSSIPFLY

Cook cautiously opened the kitchen door, brandishing her gleaming chef's knife. It trembled like an aspen leaf in the wind, betraying her nervous state. "Hello? ... Hello?"

No one was there.

KNOCK! KNOCK! The sharp rap came again.

Zackary pointed to a metallic dragonfly that bumped into the kitchen window. "Look—it's at the window."

"Oh! A Gossipfly," Cook said, her voice flooded with relief. She closed the open door and went to the window, then opened it. The Gossipfly flew into the kitchen. "Better than a Koercer, and no mistake."

The Gossipfly was a tiny drone with four silver wings and two bulbous eyes. As if doing a facial recognition scan, it checked Cook's face. Then it opened with a pop and blew a pink bubble.

Ana leaned forward curiously. The pink bubble, as large as a tire, expanded to include her. The Gossipfly delivered an audio message. The sender sounded upset.

"Cook! It's Rosalind. Have you seen Marilla's gray cat? He's gone missing. Marilla's beside herself and won't eat. It'll be no end of tears if we don't get him back. Keep an eye out for Tom, would you? If you see that rascal tomcat, send him back!"

Message delivered, the Gossipfly was spent. The pink bubble burst, splattering pink moisture everywhere, including on Cook's face. Then the Gossipfly transformed into a dormant egg-shaped object, which Cook held in her meaty hand.

Cook wiped the pink droplets from her face with the corner of her once-white apron. "Rosalind, Rosalind, Rosalind. We can't afford to waste time chasing a missing cat."

"Can I see that?" Zackary asked.

"What—this?" Cook showed Zackary the Gossipfly orb.

He reached for it, entranced. "Cool device!"

"You mustn't touch it." Cook tucked the Gossipfly into her apron pocket. "I only have one chance to send a reply."

Zackary slumped, disappointed, as he loved figuring out how machines worked. He enjoyed taking them apart and putting them back together again.

"Was that Rosalind from Bluebells Inn?" Ana asked. "The one who can locate the Wizard?"

"The very same," said Cook. "She wants help to find a missing cat. But we don't have time for such malarky."

"Yes, we do! If there's a chance we can cure my brother, we'll be glad to go hunting for a missing cat—or a missing tiger, for that matter."

Zackary gave a lop-sided grin.

"If anyone knows the whereabouts of the Wizard Snapdragon, it would be Lord Orator—but he's not here. Off on one of his trips, as usual. The next best source of information would be Mr. Berger, the owner of Bluebells Inn, and after that, my cousin Rosalind."

"Let's go to Bluebells Inn. What do you say?" Ana asked her brother.

Zackary wavered. "I'm probably going to regret this. But okay. You wished for a great role as an actor. Something that stretches you. Wish granted."

"You wished to be heroic like Percy Jackson. This is your chance to be brave. Courage is a muscle!"

"Courage is a muscle? You have such funny ideas." Zackary shook his head.

Ana turned toward Cook. "We'd like to help

Rosalind find that missing cat if we can. In return, will she provide us with directions to the Wizard Snapdragon?"

"I don't see why not," Cook said. "But you can't go dressed like that. You two stick out like tomatoes in a potato bin. Bound to get squashed. You don't want to get mistook for a witch—or a warlock."

"Do I look like a warlock?" Zackary's chest puffed out.

"That's not a good thing. People around here are suspicious of foreigners. Best to blend in."

"My sister sucks at blending in." Zackary inclined his head ruefully. "It's a problem."

Ana was stung by his words. "Every problem is an opportunity viewed inside out. Elizabeth Taylor's violet eyes made her famous."

"If Opus Die finds out about you, you'll be famous, right enough. But you won't live to see your next birthday," warned Cook.

"I'm not likely to see my next birthday in any case," muttered Zackary.

"Stop talking like that! What you think about, you bring about!"

"Stop your bellyaching and come with me." Cook steered them firmly toward the hallway. "Koercers could be here any minute. You two need proper clothes, or you'll get arrested ... or worse."

"Worse ... like what?" asked Zackary.

"Worse ... like torture, dismemberment, and a slow, agonizing death," warned Cook.

CHAPTER 15
DISGUISES

"You best leave before the Koercers arrive. Choose any clothes you like." Cook showed them a large cloakroom full of finely tailored clothes, hats, shoes, and coats. She eyed the kids for size. "Princess Margalotta left a whole pile of dresses she's outgrown. And you're about the same size as his Lordship's nephew." Cook pulled out a floor-length pink dress and held it up to Ana so that it covered her jeans and T-shirt. "That's better."

"I'm really not a dress kind of girl," Ana said.

"It wouldn't hurt you to dress up once in a while," Zackary said. "But pink is not your color. Let me see, let me see..." Zackary rummaged through the cloakroom. His tongue stuck out of this mouth in concentration.

"Best take off those cuffs. They're like a flashing sign: *I killed the Emerald Censor*," said Cook.

Ana nodded reluctantly. The bracelets were exquisite. She started unbuckling them.

Egor arrived abruptly. "Thtop! Thtop! Whatever you do, keep those cuffth on!"

"Why, Egor?" Zackary asked.

"They will protect her from the other evil Centhorth."

"Are you sure?" Cook asked.

Offended, Egor raised his unibrow. "We Glebs know a thing or two about Centhorth."

"Of course, of course, Egor," Cook said. "Look for a dress with long sleeves."

"How's Veto doing?" Ana asked.

"The little doggie ith fine." Egor beamed. "He'll be right ath clockwork in no time."

Zackary held a few dresses up to Ana's face, checking to see what suited her. "No ... No ... No ..."

Pleased with the appearance of the next dress, Zackary told her to try it.

"All right. Give me a moment. Out!" Ana shoved her brother out of the cloakroom and shut the door for privacy, which left Cook, Egor, and Zackary standing in the hallway, out of Ana's sight but within earshot.

Zackary took advantage of this opportunity to pump Egor for information. "Where's a hydrogen station, Egor?"

"Begging your pardon, young mathter. Thay again?"

"Do you know where I can refuel our hydrogen vehicle? It is out of fuel."

"It runth on hydrogen. Interethting." Egor tapped his finger on his scarred chin, wheels turning in his genius—if twisted—mind.

Later, Ana learned that most people who employed Glebs were not conventionally sane, and neither were Glebs. Sane or not, every Gleb was guaranteed to have at least one brain, and a rather clever one at that. But their sense of what was aesthetically pleasing left something to be desired, judging by the scars criss-crossing his face and arms. Fixed-pie theory, Egor had explained, by which he meant you couldn't have everything.

"What's high-drop-gents?" Cook asked.

"Hydrogen. Cleaner fuel than gasoline," Zackary explained in his lecturer voice.

"Never heard of it," said Cook.

"You use it every day. Water is two parts hydrogen, one part oxygen. H-2-O," said Zackary.

"No time to fool with recipes." Cook frowned.

Ignoring her, Egor and Zackary chatted about fuel sources, discovering a shared passion for mechanical things.

Ana emerged from the cloakroom wearing a violet

dress that accented the color of her violet eyes. "How do I look?"

"Like a beauty queen." Zackary admired his sister, who looked stunning with her long white-blonde hair, violet eyes, and the rich purple dress.

"Egad!" Cook cringed. "Your purple eyes! Those'll be the death of you. Egor, how can we hide those eyes?"

Intrigued by the challenge, Egor looked thoughtful.

"Wait a minute! Wait a minute!" Ana ducked back into the cloakroom.

While she did that, Zackary selected another dress for her. He chose an ankle-length blue velvet dress with an empire waist and long sleeves ending in a fringe of lace. Then he hunted for an outfit for himself.

Meanwhile, Cook took the Gossipfly out of her pocket. She activated it, and the Gossipfly unfolded from its dormant egg shape. She cleared her throat.

"Rosalind, it's Cook. I haven't seen Tom, but as the gods provide, an animal whisperer dropped by with her brother. They're a bit odd, but never you mind that. Foreigners, but the good kind. They're from Well-now, UK. Zorana and Zackary. They rescued our Veto today, so they're exactly what you need. I'll send them on in a jiffy."

Cook released the Gossipfly. It flew down the hallway and out through the open kitchen window.

Ana found Cook in the kitchen and spun, showing off her beautiful dress. Thanks to her colored contact lenses, her eyes were now blue, matching the dress. "How do I look?"

"Your eyes changed color! How on Tellusora did you do that?" Cook asked.

"It's a trick of the light. My eyes reflect the color of the dress," Ana lied.

Egor wasn't fooled. He peered more closely at Ana's eyes. "Ingeniouth!"

Ana turned away from Egor's scrutiny. She tied a paisley silk scarf over her hair, hiding her long white tresses.

"Ta-da!" Zackary presented himself with a flourish. He wore a chocolate-colored suit with a blue pinstripe, a white shirt buttoned to the collar, and his battered Converse high-tops. "Who do I look like?"

Without thinking, Ana tossed off, "SpongeBob SquarePants?"

Zackary gave her a scowl that said, *you may be my sister and we may be stranded in a completely unknown multiverse with only each other to rely on, but you've gone too far.* "You can do better than that."

Ana studied his outfit for a moment. "Doctor Who!"

"Very good! Which one?"

"The best one. David Tennant, of course," said Ana.

Cook beamed. "You're starting to dress like a

young lord, Zackary. But get rid of those strange shoes and cover your straw hair with a hat."

Zackary flinched, as his wispy hair was a sore spot. It still hadn't grown out properly.

"Is there a long coat?" Ana asked. "The tenth doctor had an awesome coat."

Zackary returned to the cloakroom and rummaged around. He emerged again, looking dapper in a dark-brown felt-wool flatcap. He'd added a long brown coat to his ensemble. It was too big for him, so it swept the ground theatrically. Flushed with exertion and excitement, he had a healthy glow on his usually pale cheeks.

"Outstanding," Ana said approvingly. "Time Lords, beware!"

Zackary grinned, but Cook blinked in confusion.

Ana surveyed her brother's outfit with the critical eye of someone in costume design. "Lose the cap. Doctor Who didn't wear a hat."

Zackary took off the cap, revealing his feathery blonde hair, which made him appear frail and vulnerable. He raised a questioning eyebrow at his sister. "Better?"

"Never mind. Keep the cap," said Ana decisively.

He pulled the cap over his head at a jaunty angle and twirled, which made the duster flare out dramatically.

Ana giggled in admiration. "Absolutely fantastic!"

"I haven't had this much fun in a long time!" Zackary laughed, giddy with the fun of it.

Cook handed him a pair of leather boots. "Try these on."

Zackary waved her off. "No way. The Converse are essential for pulling off the whole dapper-geek-Time-Lord look. Besides, they're comfortable."

"I'm keeping my Doc Martens, too." Ana lifted the hem of her floor-length velvet dress to reveal her prized boots.

Zackary grinned at their shared rebellion. "I like your style, Ana Banana."

She grinned back and tugged playfully on his hat. "You're looking mighty fine, Zee."

"You two could pass for a young lord and lady. At a distance," Cook said uncertainly. "If no one looks at your feet."

Ana's Doc Martens and Zackary's Converse marked them as strangers.

CHAPTER 16
OFF TO BLUEBELLS INN

A bit later, in the courtyard of Lord Orator's castle, two bay horses stood harnessed to a splendid black coach. No longer wearing scruffy jeans, Ana radiated a regal aura in her sumptuous blue dress. Long lace-trimmed sleeves hid her mysterious cuffs. A pretty paisley scarf covered her white hair, and her eyes were a brilliant blue because of her colored contact lenses.

Zackary looked dashing in the nobleman's brown suit with a blue pinstripe and a flatcap covering his hair. These clothes suited him better than the jeans and T-shirt he'd been wearing when he arrived. His long coat nearly swept the ground, but it didn't conceal his battered ivory sneakers.

Ana and her brother sauntered toward the coach. She turned up the collar of his coat. "There. You look like a badass Time Lord. All you need now is a sonic screwdriver."

Pleased, Zackary puffed up. "These clothes will be perfect for my funeral. Make a note that I want to be buried in them."

Ana flinched. "I'll do no such thing. They'll be too small for you when you're an old man."

"Always the optimist. Whereas I'm a realist."

"No, you're not. You're a pessimist. Actually, you take pessimism to a whole new level!" Ana snapped. *How can I get my brother to stop obsessing about his own death? Thoughts are things. I don't want my brother to die.*

Cook frowned as Egor arrived with Veto skipping behind him. The mostly white dog now had one chocolate-brown leg—which was incongruously longer than his three white legs.

Veto eagerly trotted up to Ana, tail wagging.

"Hello, Veto!" Ana patted the friendly, lopsided dog.

Cook scolded Egor, "I told you not to get creative! What kind of circus experiment is this? That new leg is all wrong."

"Thpare parth are hard to come by."

"Spare parts? You mean you put a spare leg on him?" Zackary asked.

"Of courthe. Otherwithe, he would run about on hith broken leg. How would it ever heal?"

Meanwhile, Veto skipped around, loving all the

attention. He seemed delighted to chase his tail—and perhaps even catch it, now that he had a leg up. Veto weaved around Ana's legs, practically tripping her. "Take me! Take me!"

Ana wondered why she was the only one who understood dog.

Cook frowned at Egor, her massive hands on her stout hips. "Lord Orator will not be pleased when he returns. He liked Veto exactly the way he was."

"Nonthenth, Cook. I'll have his leg back on by then. Good as new." To Zackary, Egor added, "Why thettle for ath good ath new? He'll be *better* than new. Of course, I'm not the Wizard Thnapdragon. Thhee would fix him up in a magical wink."

Intrigued, Zackary asked, "Do you know the Wizard Snapdragon?"

"Me? No—I've never actually *met* her. But thhe ith famouth in theeth partth." Egor swung open the chestnut carriage door, which was inlaid with honey-colored wood to create the letter O, presumably for Lord Orator. Egor held open the carriage door, waiting for Ana and Zackary to get in.

"I'd rather ride up top," Zackary said, eager for the chance to pester Egor with questions.

Egor nodded. "Ath you prefer, young mathter."

Veto took the open carriage door as an invitation. He jumped in and settled himself on the bench, looking guilty.

Ana seated herself on the dark-brown leather bench, which creaked a little. She adjusted her blue velvet dress and pulled down her sleeves to conceal the glint of gold.

The fine woodwork was polished to a high shine. The interior of the coach smelled pleasantly of leather and wood polish with a hint of horse, dog, and hay.

"Can Veto come?" Ana asked Cook.

Cook sighed as Veto grinned up at her, hope shining in his big brown eyes. His tail wagged, making a soft thumping sound against the leather bench, like the beating of a heart.

"I want to go for a ride!" Veto barked.

"Oh, all right then, Veto," Cook conceded, melting. "You win." She turned to Ana and said, "Take good care of that dog."

"I will," Ana promised. She petted Veto, glad for his company, and he wriggled in excitement.

Egor closed the coach door, and it clicked shut.

In the privacy of the coach, Ana slipped her modern journal and pen out of the worn leather shoulder bag Cook had given her in place of her modern satchel. She began to write about their astonishing multiverse adventure.

Veto nosed her, eager for attention.

She absent-mindedly stroked his silky hair. "I've got to write this down. I don't want to forget anything."

Ana heard the slap of reins, and the horse-drawn carriage rolled away.

"Bye! Thanks for everything!" Ana called to Cook from the open window.

"Bye!" Zackary called from his seat up top beside Egor.

"Try to blend in," Cook warned. That seemed odd, coming from a bossy Feinmuncher with huge hairy bare feet and toenails painted bright pink. Cook wouldn't blend in anywhere. At least not anywhere the kids had ever been.

CHAPTER 17
VETO'S SUPERPOWERS

Inside the carriage, Veto gazed up at Ana adoringly. His brown eyes melted her heart as he crept closer and put a paw on her thigh, wagging his tail. "You smell funny."

"I do?" Ana blushed and self-consciously sniffed her armpits. "I don't smell *that* bad. But this dress smells musty. I hope it's not mold. I'm allergic to mold."

Veto wriggled closer to her and put his head on her lap. "Not the dress. You. A bit like strawberries—or cherries." He sniffed her curiously. "I've never sniffed someone who smells like you before. Never ever. Why do you smell funny?"

"I've never talked to a dog before. Never ever. Why do you talk?"

"Dogs talk all the time. But masters don't listen."

Ana scratched his chest, and Veto panted contentedly.

"Maybe it's the Babbler-eel—the universal translator." She pretended to box with him.

Veto playfully boxed her hand with his paws. "I dunno."

"How come no one but me understands you?"

"You're an especially good listener," said Veto.

"Cook called me an animal whisperer."

"Are you?"

"I've always been good with animals—and I've always thought I could sense what they needed. But I've never heard a dog talk before. Not until I arrived in this strange world."

"Where did you come from?"

The carriage creaked and rocked as the horses pulled it along the dirt road. It was noisy enough to prevent anyone from eavesdropping.

"That's a bit of a story."

"Oh goodie! I like stories!" Veto sat up and looked at her eagerly, his brown eyes shining with curiosity.

"You won't believe me."

Veto raised his head inquisitively. "You say the funniest things. Dogs can sniff if a person is lying."

"Oh. I didn't know that."

"People lie all the time. You should learn to sniff better. Then you wouldn't be fooled."

Ana laughed and playfully stroked his nose. "I'll never have your acute sense of smell."

"You think my nose is cute?" Veto perked up his ears.

"Not cute—acute."

Veto dropped his ears forlornly. "You think my nose is ugly?"

"Silly! Your nose is cute. And your sense of smell is *acute*. Which is a good thing. It means really sharp."

Veto's ears pricked up. "Oh, goodie. Cute nose with a cute smell."

"Would you use that cute nose and acute sense of smell to help me?"

"Yes! Anything for master!" Veto said. "How can I help?"

"Can you tell me when someone is lying?"

"Yes! Happy to!" Veto said, thrilled to be useful. "Anything to help my pack! But I warn you: some people lie all the time."

"Hmm. We might need a code word or something." Ana drummed her fingers on the polished wooden windowsill. "Mango! That will be our code word."

"What's a mango?"

"It's a tropical fruit. But that doesn't matter. When I say 'mango,' that means I want you to tell me if someone's lying."

"Mango," Veto repeated, savoring the strange word. "Mango, mango, mango!"

Ana laughed. "Don't wear it out."

"You can wear a word out?" Veto tilted his head questioningly.

"No, it's just a silly expression."

"Oh," Veto said. "Story time! Story time! Tell me why you whiff funny!"

Ana smiled, amused by Veto's enthusiasm. "Your nose does not lie. You're right. I'm not from here. I'm from Los Angeles, California. Well, Santa Monica, actually, but everyone knows what I mean when I say LA."

"LA," Veto repeated, trying to memorize the unfamiliar name. "Is that the name of your pack? LA?"

"Hmmm. I suppose you could think of it that way. It's in the United States of America. On planet Earth. But then my brother and I moved to England to go to boarding school."

"You changed packs?"

"Sort of. Temporarily."

Veto cocked his head attentively.

"Let me see if I can explain simply so you can understand. My dad went to shoot a movie in Africa, and he decided against taking us. We're a distraction. And a liability. My brother is immune-o-compromised—"

"What's that big word mean?"

"Immunocompromised means that Zackary is super vulnerable to getting sick."

"He's the runt of the litter?"

"Hmmm ... sort of. But don't let him hear you say that!"

"He doesn't understand dog."

"Right, of course not. But you've given me a great idea for teasing him."

"I was the runt in my litter," Veto confessed sorrowfully, putting his head between his paws.

"Oh. But look what a fine dog you've grown into."

Veto gazed anxiously at her with his soulful, brown eyes. "My mother deemed I was not worthy."

"Ow. That hurts. I know, 'cause my dad thinks I'm not worthy."

Veto gave a bright bark. "Puppy fart!"

The unexpected words broke Ana's somber mood. "Puppy fart?"

"Wrong!" barked Veto.

"They're both wrong. We turned out okay," agreed Ana.

"Yes, Ana is pride of pack."

Ana beamed. "That might be stretching it."

"Story time! Story time! Why do you smell funny?"

"Right, back to my story. Dad sent us to England so we could attend Beesneese Boarding School."

"He threw you out of the pack?" Veto said, horrified.

Ana hesitated. "Maybe. I guess. He said he wanted

us to get the best education. He's busy making a movie."

"You are saying words I don't understand. What's a movie?"

"Movies are the most amazing things ever! They're like stories played by actors. Ever since I saw *The Wizard of Oz*, I decided I would be an actor, just like Judy Garland." Ana's face shone with enthusiasm.

"A human way of sharing stories?"

"Got it in one," Ana said. "Our dad shipped us off to England for boarding school. He's working in Africa, so he couldn't take care of us."

"Couldn't your mom take care of you?"

"Our mom is dead."

"Oh! So sad." Veto's brown eyes shone with love and empathy.

"It was a long time ago. When she died, I was a toddler. I barely remember her. I only remember a sweet sense of being cuddled and loved. And music. She sang to me."

"Happy memory."

"It's not much. But it's something," said Ana. "Anyway, Dad's in the film business. As he always says, 'the show must go on.' I think he was glad for an excuse to get rid of me. Perhaps he did throw me out of the pack. It seems I'm always a disappointment to him." Ana traced the runes on the cuffs with her finger. "The black sheep in the family."

Veto looked puzzled. "You have sheep in your pack?"

"No, no. It's just another expression."

"Oh. People say the funniest things."

"Anyway, my uncle—you could think of him as the leader of the pack in England—is super clever. He made this brilliant experimental car that can travel across the multiverse. And my brother and I took it for a spin—and somehow we got transported here and crashed. That's when we accidentally broke your leg."

"It's okay," Veto said. "But I miss my leg. This one makes me trip."

"I'm really sorry."

"I know. You smell truth."

"Anyway, that's when we landed on the Emerald Censor. People seem to be thrilled about that, but it was an accident. And that's how I got these." Ana showed the cuffs around her wrists. "The Emerald Censor's cuffs."

"Spicy!"

"I wish I knew exactly what they do. Anyway, the main thing is we need to find the Wizard Snapdragon, so she can make my brother better. So that's our mission. Worthy or not, here we come!"

"I'll protect you, master!" Veto said valiantly.

"I wish you wouldn't call me that."

"What? Calling you master is love and respect."

"It sounds bad where I come from."

Veto cocked his head quizzically. "What should I call you?"

"Ana."

"I'll try to remember. I'll watch your back, mast—I mean, Ana."

"Thanks." Ana grinned and stroked his silky, soft fur. "And we'd better have these long talks when we're alone. Otherwise, people will guess that you're my secret protector."

"Secret protector!" Veto puffed out his chest. "Wow! Can I get a vest or badge?"

"If you do a good job, I'm sure I can come up with something."

"Your secret protector. Wow!" Veto sat up straight and it seemed he might burst with pride. "Everyone else thinks I'm too little to do anything useful."

"Well, we know that's not true, don't we?"

"Yes, we do!"

"Who's a good dog?" Ana said, fussing over him.

"I am! I am!" Veto's tail thumped happily against the bench.

"You are a good dog!" Ana crooned.

"Can the Wizard heal my leg?"

"I don't see why not. If she can heal Zackary, why not you too?"

"Take me with you! Take me with you!"

"All right. We're off to see the Wizard …" Ana fondly remembered playing the Wicked Witch in her school performance of *The Wizard of Oz*. She hummed a few bars of "We're Off to See the Wizard."

Veto perked up and wagged his tail to the beat. The carriage slowed and rolled to a stop as it arrived at their destination. Ana gazed eagerly out the window, full of anticipation.

What will happen next?

CHAPTER 18
VETO WARNS OF DANGER

BLUEBELLS INN, PROSPERUS, TELLUSORA.

Bluebells Inn was a three-story, ivy-laced brick building with perhaps thirty rooms, a pub, stables, and a large garden. The coach slowed and then stopped in the courtyard.

"Showtime!" Ana announced, then opened the carriage door to make a dramatic entrance. She always got a thrill when she was performing in a play. You had to sell it to the audience, and with live theater there were no second takes. So she was eager to assume her role as an eccentric animal whisperer and distant cousin to Lord Orator. This would be fun.

Rosalind bustled out of the inn to greet them, wiping her hands on her apron. A Feinmuncher like her cousin Cook, Rosalind was plump. Like Cook, she had a friendly, rosy face. Unlike Cook, she appeared defeated rather than defiant. Her huge hairy feet were bare, and her toenails were painted copper, which was slightly more alluring than the brash pink Cook favored.

Egor, Ana, and Zackary descended from the coach to greet Rosalind. Veto trailed behind, exploring all the stimulating scents.

"Hello, Egor. Nice to see you again." Rosalind cowered as Egor towered over her. Evidently, they did not share the same warm camaraderie as Cook and Egor.

"Rothalind," acknowledged Egor.

"And you must be Zorana, the animal whisperer?"

"That's right." Mixing the truth brazenly with lies, Ana said, "Please forgive our foreign ways. We're not from around here. I'm Zorana, the animal whisperer. This is my brother, Zackary."

"We need hydrogen for our car. Where's the nearest hydrogen refueling station?" asked Zackary.

Rosalind blinked in confusion. "You need what for what?"

"Hydrogen. For our car."

"Your car? What's a car?"

"You know, four wheels, drives on the freeway ..."

Rosalind seemed lost at sea.

Ana glared at Zackary and hissed, "Improv, Zee, improv!" To Rosalind, she added, "He's always on about machines. He's more of a machine whisperer, you could say."

Rosalind's eyes narrowed suspiciously. "An animal whisperer and a machine whisperer? You don't say."

"Pleased to meet you, I'm sure, Zorana and Zackary." Rosalind frowned as she noticed the little dog. "What's wrong with his leg?"

Veto skipped about enthusiastically, sniffing everywhere. He didn't seem to care that his three white legs were shorter than his one brown leg.

"It's in the thop. For repair," said Egor.

"Oh ... well," Rosalind said uncertainly.

"We can't have him running about on a broken leg. It wouldn't heal properly." Zackary looked up at Egor, who nodded approvingly at his student.

"Right, then." Rosalind steered the conversation back to more certain ground. "Thank you for coming. Marilla's all a-tizzy about her missing cat. I'd be ever so grateful if you could find him. Oh! Where are my manners? I'm Rosalind, the cook at Bluebells Inn. Come in, come in!"

They followed Rosalind toward the inn. She shambled, laboring to breathe. "I can't seem to catch my breath these days. It's like the air has gone all thin."

"It mutht be the fireth. Thmoke everywhere." Egor moved from discussing the weather to shop talk—at least for Glebs. "We Glebs have theen a thpike in demand for thpare lungs."

"Spare lungs?" Zackary asked, surprised. "Whoever has spare lungs?"

"You have *two*, you know," Egor said, as if that explained everything.

"Rosalind, Cook said you might know how we can find the Wizard Snap—" Ana started.

"Danger! Danger!" Veto barked urgently.

Ana whirled. Two steaming dapple-gray horses raced into the courtyard, pulling a coach. The foam-flecked horses barreled straight toward them, hooves pounding.

"Watch out!" warned Ana, pulling her brother out of the way.

Egor whisked the rotund Feinmuncher to safety. Veto scampered out of danger.

"Really!" Rosalind tut-tutted, wheezing. "Some people!"

"I have cute hearing," Veto told Ana proudly.

"Good dog," said Ana, relieved. "That was close!"

"Danger!" Veto growled, hackles rising. "Predator!"

CHAPTER 19
How Do You Make a Puppet?

The coach rolled to a sudden stop, dust billowing, as the steaming horses were reined in suddenly. The horses tossed their manes, and their bridles jingled. The coach had a distinctive coat of arms: a round bubble with a pointy tail—the mirror image of a capital Q—canceled out with a slash.

"A Centhor," warned Egor.

"Another one?" Ana's face drained of color.

"It's not thafe for you here. Be careful. Don't thay anything ... provocative," said Egor.

"Provocative? What's provocative?" Zackary frowned.

But Egor had already vanished.

"You'll pretty much have to keep quiet. Everything you say is provocative, Zackary," Ana joked, but the joke landed flat as her voice was strained with worry.

"Funny, coming from the Fibbermeister," grumbled Zackary.

Ignoring his insult, Ana scooped up the lapdog and cuddled him. "Good boy." As she did so, the cuffs shimmered in the sunshine.

Zackary protectively pulled her lace-edged sleeves down over her cuffs to conceal them. "Careful."

"Thanks, Zee," Ana whispered. Veto growled at Zackary, taking his role as guard dog seriously, undeterred by his diminutive size. "Shh, Veto."

Ana cringed as they skirted past the coach, following Rosalind past a few other startled people, including the doorman, gardener, and several inn guests, including a mother and toddler.

Rosalind disappeared into Bluebells Inn.

Before the kids could follow her, a big, beefy man angrily pushed his way out of the inn, momentarily blocking their entry. Later, they learned he was the inn's owner, Mr. Berger. The kids hesitated in the shadows cast by the awning and turned to gawk at the confrontation.

Mr. Berger ran toward the coach, his face red with fury. "Hey! No reckless driving! How many times do I have to tell you?" Mr. Berger angrily confronted the carriage driver and captain, both of whom wore the gray uniform of Opus Die.

The driver dismissed his complaint mechanically. "We obey Brightness Cacophony, not you."

This infuriated Mr. Berger, and his ruddy face and neck flushed even redder. "This is my inn! You'll do as I say! Or leave!"

Ignoring Mr. Berger, the captain descended stiffly to open the carriage door, his face blank and swirls of woodgrain on his cheeks revealing that he was made of wood.

Ana elbowed her brother and whispered, "A wooden man!"

Zackary raised his eyebrows in surprise as Ana snapped a few photos of the surprising scene with her smartphone.

The Crimson Censor, magnificently attired in a scarlet dress that showed off her slender waist, descended gracefully from the coach. Ana glimpsed red soles on her black stilettos. Her flaming hair was crowned with a stylish white-and-black fur hat adorned with scarlet feathers. The smooth skin on her ivory face suggested she was about thirty.

Mr. Berger cringed as he confronted the scarlet sorceress, but he plowed on. This was his inn, after all. "You must slow down! There are children about. We don't want any accidents."

Ignoring him, the Crimson Censor (also known as Brightness Cacophony) snapped, "What do you know about the murder of my sister, the Emerald Censor?"

"What? The Emerald Censor is dead?" Mr. Berger's shock turned to surprise, then satisfaction.

Crimson's eyes narrowed. "You sound happy."

"Best news I've heard in a long time." Mr. Berger's smile grew wide.

"I know all about you, Mr. Berger. I know you have an ax to grind. Did you kill her?"

"She killed my son. The world is better off without her—and her kind," Mr. Berger said unwisely.

"Show me your wrists, Mr. Berger," Crimson commanded.

"What? Why?"

Crimson snatched up his hands and examined his hairy wrists. He wore a braided leather bracelet on one wrist, but no golden cuffs. She snorted and tossed his hands away like garbage.

"The murderer stole cuffs, like these." She presented her wrists with the burnished bracelets covered with runes and studded with tiny rubies. "Have you seen anyone wearing cuffs like these?" Crimson glared at Mr. Berger, then her eyes swept over the frightened onlookers, who cowered and shook their heads.

Ana shrank deeper into the shadows where she and Zackary had lingered to observe. Ana held her breath and clenched her sleeves to her wrists, concealing the Emerald Censor's cuffs.

If anyone sees these, I'm done for!

Crimson's eyes swept past Ana, the gardener frozen in fright, the cowering doorman, and several intimidated guests. She narrowed her eyes. "Well? I haven't got all day, Mr. Berger. Have you spotted anyone wearing golden cuffs?"

"No—and I wouldn't tell you if I did. The Bluebells Inn welcomes all travelers—no matter the species, no matter what odd clothes or jewelry they're wearing. We respect people's customs, possessions, and privacy."

"How quaint. And outdated. Get with the times. I am the *only* one you need to respect. Are you harboring the murderer?"

"How by Opus Die would I know? We don't search people when they check into Bluebells Inn."

"From now on, you will interrogate, search, and report the identity of every traveler to me."

"What? Absolutely not! My inn is a sanctuary—not an outstation for your Koercers!"

"Every place, every person, serves me. And my conscripted Koercers."

"*Your* Koercers? I thought you all served our Lord Opus Die."

Ana winced, as he'd clearly gone too far.

"We *all* serve Opus Die, but *your* service is dismally deficient." Crimson's square jaw flexed as she ground her teeth. "Long live Opus Die."

"Long live Opus Die," chorused the onlookers automatically.

The porter noticed that neither Ana nor Zackary chimed in, and he frowned and narrowed his eyes. Realizing they weren't safe, Ana pulled her brother deeper into the shadows.

Crimson tapped her cuffs smartly together, making a ringing sound that hung in the air. She muttered an incantation and Mr. Berger shimmered and transformed into a man-sized wooden puppet. His ruddy skin became grainy wood.

He blinked, stupefied. Everyone in the courtyard took a step back and gasped. The porter was agape at the sight of his employer reduced to a ridiculous puppet.

The Crimson Censor commanded, "Kneel."

Mr. Berger kneeled, heedless of the dirt.

"Bow."

Mr. Berger bowed until his wooden forehead touched the dirt.

"Grovel."

Mr. Berger forlornly apologized for the act of being—for taking up space, time, and air. He continued to mutter a stream of incoherent apologies, crawling in the dirt, heedless of the mud on his trousers and wooden hands.

"Beg for mercy."

Mr. Berger begged for mercy, mumbling a litany of

requests for her to be merciful and save his worthless life, to spare his innocent daughter and industrious wife. His bald head shone like polished furniture as he begged for her to have mercy on Bluebells Inn and all the travelers who sheltered there.

Crimson's eyes narrowed, and her mouth twisted into a sneer. She folded her arms and looked away in irritation. Bored with her display of power, she snapped, "Stand up."

Mr. Berger creaked as he stood, wiping his muddy hands on his trousers. He slumped in defeat—no longer a man full of vim and vigor, but her slave.

"You see? Obedience is not optional." Once again, the Crimson Censor's eyes scanned the frightened onlookers. The lesson was not lost on them. Some made a sign of protection over their hearts: a circle with a slash, the symbol of Opus Die.

Hidden in shadow, Ana watched, her heart racing. For one insane moment, her rebellious nature urged her to stand up and speak out against the Censor, but the wiser part of her curbed that insane impulse. She sought her brother's gaze and saw he, too, was appalled.

"Come on." Zackary jerked his head, urging her into the inn.

Despite her rising terror, Ana turned back to watch the unfolding drama, unable to tear herself away.

The Crimson Censor turned her attention back to

Mr. Berger. In a hypnotic voice, she commanded, "I will prepare the best suite for you."

Mr. Berger repeated, "I will prepare the best suite for you."

"I will prepare the finest food for you and your entourage."

Mr. Berger repeated woodenly, "I will prepare the finest food for you and your entourage."

"On the house, of course, to thank you for all that you do."

"On the house, of course, to thank you for all that you do," he repeated dully.

"Now go about your business before I turn you into firewood. Chop-chop!"

Mr. Berger blinked and seemed to rouse himself from a daydream. He snapped at the porter, "Hurry, man, hurry! The Censor doesn't have all day! Chop-chop!"

The porter closed his open mouth and hurried to work. A great deal of expensive luggage—monogrammed with her initials, CC—accompanied her.

The Crimson Censor thrust a cloaked birdcage into Mr. Berger's wooden hands. "Take special care of my parrot."

Mr. Berger took it stiffly. "I am at your service."

"I know," she said smugly, tossing her luxuriant red hair over her shoulder.

CHAPTER 20
WE'VE GOT TO GET OUT OF HERE

Shaken by what they had witnessed, Ana and Zackary shared a troubled glance. The inn promised a safe haven, so they slipped deeper into it, unsure of what awaited them. The multiverse was exciting—but it also held unpredictable dangers.

They entered the spacious foyer, which had mustard-colored walls. The pine floor creaked underfoot. It was marred by the footsteps of countless travelers. The inn smelled musty, with lingering scents of fish and ale. They ducked into a dimly lit hallway.

"We've got to get out of here before Cruella de Vil sees your cuffs and turns you into a wooden puppet," said Zackary.

"She seems more like Maleficent to me." Ana added, mimicking the Crimson Censor, "Obedience is not optional."

Her imitation of Crimson's voice was rather good, and Zackary shifted uneasily. "Whatever. Pick your villain. Look, this is as good a place to die as any—for me, I mean. But we need hydrogen to get you home."

"We only just arrived. We need the Wizard to heal you. Don't you see that's the reason the multiverse app sent us to this place?"

"What? You're such a dreamer!"

"Everything happens for a reason," said Ana.

"Hogwash." Zackary rolled his eyes.

"Why are you always such a wet blanket?" said Ana.

"I'm being a realist. The multiverse is random chaos."

"No, it isn't. There's a hidden pattern to everything. Everything is connected to everything else. We were sent here on purpose to heal you. We have to find that Wizard."

"And you know this because ...?" Zackary said incredulously.

"I just do. I feel it in my bones," Ana said with conviction.

Zackary raised a disbelieving eyebrow.

Rosalind opened the door leading into the kitchen and waved at them urgently. "This way, this way!"

Ana waved back and started toward her. She whispered to her brother, "Now play along and don't blow our cover. It's showtime!"

Ana had that old electric sensation, the one she got when she stood on stage and the spotlight focused on her. It was the thrill of being so perfectly in character that the universe held its breath and the audience bought every line. It was the rush of being so believable that you could fool the world and spin it on your finger ... at least for one scene. She thrived in moments like these, when her thoughts flowed like quicksilver.

Rosalind fussed about, her nerves frayed. The Bluebells Inn kitchen was larger but plainer than the one at Lord Orator's castle. The plates were plain crockery, not fancy china, and the black pots and pans were scratched with hard use, not lustrous copper. Another door led outside to the kitchen gardens, and large double doors led into the dining area.

The kids plopped down on sturdy wooden chairs beside a plank table that was worn but scrupulously clean. Veto nestled in Ana's arms, looking around with interest.

"May Opus Die protect us." Rosalind made a sign to ward off evil—but it was the symbol of Opus Die—a circle with a slash.

"May Opus Die protect us," repeated Ana, mimicking Rosalind's motion, playing her role. "To do my job as an animal whisperer, I need all the facts about your missing cat."

"Of course. I'll get Marilla." Rosalind lumbered to open the hallway door, wheezing. She called, "Marilla!" She clumped back to inspect the baking in the twin wood-burning ovens.

"Who was that? That man turned into a wooden puppet?" Ana asked.

"Mr. Berger, the owner." Rosalind opened the oven door and withdrew several golden-brown loaves. The scent of freshly baked bread made Ana's mouth water.

"Will Mr. Berger be okay? Will he become a real man again?" Ana asked.

Rosalind checked a tray of cinnamon buns and slid them out of the oven. Spatula quivering, Rosalind freed the steaming buns from the tray. Keeping busy seemed to calm her shattered nerves. Finally, she said reluctantly, "I've never heard of a Censor turning someone back."

"That's evil!" Ana gasped.

"Hush now." Rosalind's voice was laced with fear. Clearly, she was used to keeping her head down and her mouth shut.

"But it's true! Right, Veto?" said Ana.

"Right!" Veto agreed, wagging his tail.

Zackary snorted scornfully.

"No naming things. Naming things makes them real, calls them forth." Rosalind took comfort in reciting a slogan. "If you can't say it, then you can't think it. If you can't think it, then you can't have a problem."

She slid one bun each onto three small plates and

ferried the plates toward the table on a tray. Noticing Zackary's dusty cream Converse high-tops, she frowned. "Odd shoes. I've never seen the likes of them."

"Standard issue for animal whisperers. The special footwear helps him be as quiet as a cat," Ana invented. She was good at keeping her body calm, but her anxiety showed up in her twitching foot, which revealed the shiny black leather toe of her Doc Martens peeking out from under the hem of her dress.

"But you're wearing boots," Rosalind observed.

"Ideal for dealing with horses and cows and the like," invented Ana. She loved her boots—they made her feel invulnerable.

Rosalind set out three plates with steaming cinnamon buns, and the scent was enticing. "Eat! Where's that girl? Never comes when I call her." Rosalind lumbered heavily to the hallway door, opened it, and called out, "Marilla! Marilla Berger!"

Ana took a bite, which melted in her mouth. "Mmm!"

Zackary absentmindedly straightened the three plates.

"You should eat something. You know how you get when you've got low blood sugar."

Repulsed by the sight of food, Zackary pushed his plate away. "How can you eat at a time like this?"

CHAPTER 21
MEETING MARILLA

"Come on, eat something," Ana coaxed, pushing the plate toward her brother. "You look terrible."

"Thanks," Zackary said, but he relented and nibbled on the cinnamon bun. "Not bad."

"Not bad?" Offended, Rosalind tapped one enormous hairy bare foot, and her copper toenails came across as pennies bouncing up and down.

"The best I've ever tasted," Ana said.

"Of course. I'm a Feinmuncher," huffed Rosalind, mollified.

"And I'm an animal whisperer. Tell us everything you know about the missing cat." Ana pitched her voice right, so she sounded like she knew what she was doing, like she'd done this dozens of times before.

But, as usual, she was winging it. These were the

moments she lived for, the thrill of improv, the challenge of pretending to be someone else so completely that she lost herself in the role and the only thing that was real was this very moment. Action ... reaction. Offer and acceptance. Her acting coach would be proud of her.

"Tom's an indoor cat. Not much of a ratter," Rosalind said disapprovingly.

"Is that still important? Haven't we got bigger problems than finding a stupid cat?" Zackary's pale face was gradually regaining color. "The sorceress turned the inn owner into a puppet!"

"Don't talk about that." Rosalind glanced about nervously, but there was no one else in the kitchen. Once again, she made the sign to ward off evil. "Finding that cat *is v*ital. When Marilla gets upset, she can't breathe. She turns blue."

"An asthma attack. I've had those myself." Ana chewed on her lower lip.

Ana had been rushed to the hospital several times with life-threatening asthma attacks. The air in L.A. wasn't great at the best of times, and if the pollen count was especially high, or there was a wildfire or weird weather inversion, she could be in jeopardy. She remembered her fingernails turning blue and fighting for every ragged breath, slowly suffocating, until the doctors had saved her.

"It's causing me no end of tears. The Bergers lost

their son. I can't imagine what they'd do if they lost their daughter, too." Rosalind took a labored breath to calm her nerves.

"She turned that man into her slave—" started Zackary.

Rosalind slammed her hairy foot against the floor with a thud, drowning out Zackary's words. "Shut up!"

Startled by Rosalind's vehemence, Zackary abruptly shut his mouth.

"I'm sorry to be so rude, but you don't understand. You *have to* stop talking like that. It's not safe. Plus, you mustn't worry the innkeeper's daughter." Rosalind's face became flushed. "That's important. Or it'll be my head for listening to Cook and inviting you here."

Just then, a five-year-old girl wearing a blue gingham dress trotted into the kitchen. Her dark-brown hair framed her face in two long braids tied at the ends with pink ribbons.

"Here she is now. Marilla Berger," Rosalind announced, a steely edge in her tone of voice that warned the kids not to upset her delicate charge.

Marilla saw the dog sitting on Ana's lap and made a beeline toward him.

"What a cute dog!" Marilla patted Veto, who sniffed her curiously. "What's his name?"

"This is Veto," said Ana.

"Hello, little doggie!" Marilla fussed over him, then peeked coyly at Zackary.

"Smells of cat," Veto said.

"Marilla, these are the animal whisperers I told you about. They're going to find Tom," Rosalind said.

"Hi Marilla, I'm Zorana." Ana smiled warmly.

"And I'm Zackary. Still." Zackary sighed despondently, seemingly unhappy to find himself still trapped in his frail body.

Ana pursed her lips.

"Hi." Marilla slipped onto the chair beside Zackary and ate her sticky bun by peeling it open then eating the ribbon of warm, sugary bread. "Can you find my cat?"

"Of course. That's why we're here." Ana placed Veto on the floor so he could explore. He was in doggie heaven exploring all the scents. But gold glinted at Ana's wrists.

Zackary flashed a warning glare at his sister and touched Marilla's shoulder to distract her attention. "Tell us about your cat."

Ana tugged at the lace-fringed sleeves of her dress and concealed the incriminating cuffs once again.

"He's gray. And he loves me." Marilla looked adoringly at Zackary.

Ana felt bemused that the little girl seemed enchanted by her annoying brother. She tilted her head and peered at her brother with fresh eyes. She supposed her green-eyed blonde brother was sort of good-looking—in a slender, elfin way. *Does that mean he's getting healthier?*

"Can you show us his favorite places, Marilla?" Ana asked.

Marilla nodded. Still eating her cinnamon bun, she slid off the chair. "Come on! This way!" she put her sticky hand in Zackary's, leading the way.

He seemed both surprised and grossed out by her affection and sticky hand. "Lead the way," he said, reclaiming his hand and wiping it on his trousers.

Ana held back for a moment to tell Rosalind, "We need to find the Wizard."

"Which one?" asked Rosalind.

Ana blinked, surprised there was more than one. "The Wizard Snapdragon. How can we find him? Or her? Or them?"

Rosalind frowned at the odd request. "I don't know—but perhaps I could ask Mr. Berger for you. He might know."

"Do you *promise* to ask him?" Ana pestered.

"If you find the cat, I'll ask."

"Promise?" Ana badgered.

"I promise. Get on with you now." Rosalind crossed her ample arms, exasperated, and tapped her huge hairy foot, copper toenails glimmering.

Ana spun on her heel and hurried to catch up to Zackary, Veto, and Marilla, who were in the hallway.

Mr. Berger poked his wooden head in the other kitchen door, startling Rosalind. Knots and wood grain showed on his face and hands. "The Crimson Censor wants her afternoon tea. Chop-chop!"

Ana melted out the far door without attracting Mr. Berger's angry eyes.

"Yes, sir," Rosalind said, her voice squeaking with fright. "Coming right up."

CHAPTER 22
WHAT'S BEHIND THAT DOOR?

Whenever they arrived at a locked door, Marilla opened it with the master keys hanging from a silver chain around her neck. She escorted Ana and Zackary through the maze of corridors in Bluebells Inn, chattering away to Veto, who eagerly explored scents.

Marilla skipped ahead and recited in a singsong voice,

> *"An age-old Prophecy, whispered and told,*
> *Of two siblings from a land afar, bold,*
> *Both with snowy-white hair, a sight to behold,*
> *One hears the language of animals, we're told,*

*The other understands machines with
   great ease,
Their bond entwined, as the Prophecy
   decrees ..."*

Zackary whispered, "What's the plan, Ana Banana?"

"Let's keep a low profile. Do as expected. No one will suspect two of Marilla's friends."

"Unless they see those cuffs."

"Shh!" Ana frowned and checked that her cuffs were concealed.

On the third floor, Marilla led them down a corridor toward her playroom, room 35.

The porter labored past them, bringing Crimson's monogrammed luggage into her suite, room 33.

"Thank you. That will be all," she said dismissively. She shut the door in the porter's face as he blathered on about being at her service.

Marilla unlocked the door to the adjacent room, then tucked the keys back under her cotton dress, which had a blue-and-white checkered pattern. Her playroom was full of toys, dolls, and stuffed animals. Marilla's childish drawings hung from clothes pegs on strings along one wall. Some were charcoal on scrolls, others were brightly painted.

"Come see!" Marilla pointed at one series of scribbles. "The life cycle of a dragon. See?"

"Oh, yes, wonderful," Zackary said generously. "Tell me about it."

Marilla prattled, enjoying the attention of the intriguing boy as she pointed out things on her drawings. "That's the egg. See, it's hatching here. That's the juvenile. And see here? That's the full-grown, fire-breathing dragon!"

"You have dragons here?" Zackary asked, intrigued.

"Not here. Mommy and Daddy won't allow me to have one for a pet," Marilla complained.

"*Really?* I can't imagine why not," Zackary said sarcastically. The girl was clearly spoiled, but sarcasm was lost on her.

"Me, either," she said, beaming.

The kids hunted everywhere for the cat, searching behind dolls, teddy bears, and an elaborate doll's house. Marilla's room had a bunk bed for sleepovers, and her bed had a pink bedspread that made Ana think of a fancy cake with icing.

Veto explored under the bed and came out wearing a dust bunny on his nose. He sneezed. "Dusty!"

"Silly puppy." Ana gently removed the dust bunny from Veto's nose.

"Cat smell is old."

"Who's a good boy?" Ana crooned.

"I am! I am!" Veto said, his feathery white tail

wagging as it curled over his back. Veto grinned up at her, and his liquid brown eyes melted her heart.

Marilla brought Ana a bracelet with tiny glass beads on an elastic string. "This is for you. I made it." Marilla rolled the homemade bracelet over Ana's wrist until it lay right beside the cuff.

Ana could have kicked herself for letting Marilla see the Emerald Censor's golden cuff. She had to stay in character—and stay out of trouble.

"Are these magic?" Marilla asked, tracing a rune on one mysterious cuff.

Ana floundered. "Can you keep a secret?"

"Oh, yes!" Marilla twisted one heel up and swept it back and forth, eager to learn a secret.

"Mango!" barked Veto. "She smells of lies."

Even though Marilla was a little girl, she had a big mouth, according to Veto.

The bracelet of glass beads was too small for Ana's wrist, and it was cutting off the circulation. But she didn't want to hurt Marilla's feelings, so she wrapped it around her thumb. "Thank you. It makes a lovely ring."

"Tell me the secret," said Marilla as she caressed the cuff.

"They help me tune into an animal's frequency," invented Ana. "So I can find lost pets more easily."

"Show me! How do they work?"

"Uh ..." said Ana.

"Your cat's not here," Zackary announced, interrupting the girls. Ana shot him a grateful glance.

"I know. I looked a dozen times already. But you'll find Tom with these magic cuffs!"

"Hush now. Don't tell anyone about my cuffs," said Ana seriously.

"Why not?" Marilla pouted.

"Uh ... people will steal them. Then I won't be able to find your cat. And you wouldn't want that, would you?"

"No." Marilla traced the runes on the cuffs. "They're so pretty. Can I wear one?"

"Not right now. I need them to do my work as an animal whisperer. Excuse me." Ana escaped the meddlesome child and fled to the balcony.

The balcony was long and narrow, spanning both Marilla's room and the one next door. At one time, both rooms had been part of one larger suite. Veto trotted behind her. He tilted his head quizzically as Ana searched behind some potted plants.

A raucous voice startled Ana. It declared, "Time is a persistent illusion."

Peeking into the adjacent suite, Ana observed the Crimson Censor open the birdcage and then snap her fingers twice. The parrot responded to this signal and settled on Crimson's shoulder.

Crimson commanded, "Apertus!"

The air shimmered. Did something shift?

Ana took a step away from the window, her heart thumping wildly, anxious to remain unseen. But her curiosity was stronger than her fear, and she continued to observe from her hiding place.

Her skirts rustling, the scarlet sorceress strode toward the wardrobe, which flanked the exterior wall of Bluebells Inn. She opened the armoire door, and something inside lit up her pale but beautiful face.

The parrot bobbed its head up and down, glaring at Ana. But its mistress remained oblivious to Ana's presence.

Fully dressed, right down to her boots and her fur hat, the Crimson Censor stepped into the wardrobe—and shut the door behind her.

Perplexed, Ana tried to make sense of what she had just seen. *How peculiar! Who stands inside an armoire?* The wardrobe stood against the outside wall of the third story of the brick building. The Crimson Censor couldn't have gone anywhere. Unless …

CHAPTER 23
SAVE THE CAT

Ana ducked back into Marilla's playroom, Veto at her heels. "I saw the oddest thing ..."

No one paid any attention to her. Marilla was distraught, and Zackary was being logical rather than comforting.

"Run over by a coach—or eaten by a coyote. Might as well face facts. Your cat's a goner," Zackary said glumly.

"A goner?" Marilla cried.

"Dead," Zackary said.

Marilla started crying in great gasps. "D-d-dead?"

"Not helpful!" Ana said.

Zackary shrugged. "The truth hurts, but it heals."

"That's not the *truth*—that's your *theory*. Stop being such a pessimist."

"Realist," Zackary countered.

Marilla started turning blue from lack of oxygen.

Veto tried to comfort her by pushing his nose into her lap. "There, there."

"Why did you upset her, Zackary? You've triggered an asthma attack. Her fingernails are turning blue."

The more Marilla panicked, the worse it got. "I can't breathe ... I can't breathe ..."

"There, there now. Everything's going to be all right. My brother was teasing you. You know how boys are—they never know when to stop." Ana glared at her brother.

She gathered the distressed little girl in her arms and paced around, soothing her. "We'll find your cat. Animal whisperers never fail. It's against our code of conduct. Do you understand how animal whisperers work?"

In Ana's comforting arms, Marilla's panic eased, and she became curious. "No."

"I hear the animals whispering, and then I whisper back to them," Ana invented, her voice becoming softer and softer. "And how can you hear a whisper?"

"I have to be quiet and listen." Marilla grew quiet so she could hear Ana's whispered words.

"Exactly! You're a clever girl, Marilla. Let's all listen and see if we can hear your cat," whispered Ana.

Marilla strained to listen and Veto pricked up his ears. For a moment, everything was peaceful.

"I don't hear anything," said Marilla.

"Clean the wax out of your ears," teased Zackary.

"I don't have wax in my ears!"

"Shush!" Ana said.

They all concentrated on listening.

"I hear cat!" Veto barked, breaking the silence.

"Veto heard your cat. We animal whisperers use trained canines to help us locate lost animals," Ana guessed.

Zackary raised an eyebrow, but he played along to keep Marilla from having another asthma attack.

With his peculiar lopsided gait, Veto padded to the door and scratched it.

"Let's go. Lead the way, Veto," Ana said.

Marilla wiped away her tears, calm once again, so Ana put her down. Marilla grabbed her teddy bear for moral support.

Zackary opened the door, and Veto scooted out, leading the way. They all followed him down the hallway.

Marilla twisted her finger in her ear to clean the wax out of it. She pulled out a big yellow gob of earwax, which she flung onto the carpet with disgust. "Ew!"

"Told you so," said Zackary.

Veto sniffed the glob of earwax.

"Veto, no!" Ana said.

"Candy?" Veto wagged his tail, interested.

"Not candy—earwax. Leave it," said Ana.

"Oh, all right, master." Veto reluctantly left the intriguing lump of earwax.

"Don't call me master. Call me Ana," Ana rebuked Veto.

"I'll try to remember," said Veto sheepishly.

"Good boy. Find the cat!" urged Ana.

Veto raced ahead, and Marilla followed close behind.

Zackary, who didn't understand dog, arched an eyebrow at his sister. "Don't you think you're taking this whole animal whisperer thing a bit far? I know you love acting, but you don't have to pretend to have conversations with a dog to impress me and Marilla."

"I'm not pretending. I *can* understand him."

Zackary snorted skeptically. "Yeah, right."

"Just because you can't do something doesn't mean I can't do it. We're different."

"That's an understatement." Zackary opened his mouth to continue, but shut it as they caught up to Marilla. He apparently didn't want to blow their cover by arguing about Earth.

Veto pawed at the closed door leading into the stairwell.

"Find the cat, Veto. Use your acute hearing and sense of smell!" Ana said encouragingly.

"I have a cute hearing and smell," Veto said proudly, wagging his tail.

Marilla opened the door, and the kids wound

down the stairs, following Veto. Veto scampered ahead, and Marilla raced excitedly after him, her footsteps echoing in the stairwell. This gave Ana and Zackary a moment to talk privately.

"Let's not argue," said Ana. "We have to stick together and be a team."

"Ana Banana, as much as I hate to admit it …" He paused and grinned his winning lopsided smile. "You're right."

"Of course I'm right. Listen up, Zee." Ana told her brother all about the odd sight she had seen: the Crimson Censor, fully dressed, walking into the wardrobe and vanishing. "Maybe it's a portal," Ana said eagerly.

"Unlikely." Zackary's brow furrowed into a disbelieving frown. "She was probably changing her clothes."

"No way. She was already dressed. Right down to her coat and boots! And the parrot was perched on her shoulder. If it's a portal, perhaps we can use it to get back home," Ana said hopefully.

"Ever the optimist."

"Optimists have more fun!"

"Even if it *is* a portal—which is highly unlikely—there's a million-to-one chance it will take us back home," said Zackary.

"You know what they say about million-to-one chances?"

"No—what?"

"They always happen!"

"That makes no mathematical sense. None." Zackary shook his head.

The kids followed Marilla and Veto and arrived at the mammoth wooden door of the inn's larder. Veto whined and pawed at the closed door.

"Is the cat in here, Veto?"

With effort, Ana opened the massive door to the cold storage room in the cellar of Bluebells Inn. It opened with a groan, revealing …

CHAPTER 24
THE SECRET MULTIVERSE ACADEMY

CROWNED CITADEL, REXHAVEN, AVENIR.

In a high-tech room protected by the bio-dome, a breathtakingly beautiful boy sat on a dark-green leatherette couch, a sleek controller in hand. Flickering light from monitors cast an eery light on the boy's ivory face and full lips.

Prince Hunter concentrated on the video game he was playing. "She's so controlling! I can't stand it!"

"How did it go when you tried nonviolent communication?" the AI Therapist, N2ME-C, asked in her usual tone of neutral curiosity. Her attractive face conveyed empathy.

They were alone in a sleek, high-tech room containing several large monitors. One monitor revealed a lively video game with attacking armies and the fog of war. Others revealed video surveillance of

Tellusora from a dozen raven sims perched in trees or on buildings.

"I can never remember to do that in the heat of the moment," admitted Prince Hunter.

"Let's role-play. Can you identify what needs are not being met?" N2ME-C said.

"Freedom! Respect! Choice! Independence!" said Prince Hunter.

"Quite a few."

"I could go on. I never get to do what I want. She's impossible."

"Do you remember the four steps of nonviolent communication?" asked the AI therapist.

"Let me see, first I—" Prince Hunter began.

The door banged open, and Queen Crimson swept in. Her head was adorned with a sophisticated white and black fur hat, accented by striking scarlet plumes.

She peeled off her fur coat and gloves, revealing her powerful cuffs. "Report!"

"Hey! Can't you see the red light is on? How about not interrupting *my* therapy session?" Prince Hunter protested, gesturing at the illuminated red light by the door frame.

"Don't be absurd. I'm back from Tellusora."

"We call it Lokey," groused Hunter.

"Opus Die calls it Tellusora now, and so do we." Queen Crimson clicked off the video game. "Report."

"Mom!" Hunter protested. "I'm in the middle of a game."

"And now you are not. Time to report to your queen. Status update." Queen Crimson picked up her tiara from the counter and placed it on her head with a sigh of satisfaction. "Born to rule."

"Prince Hunter has something he'd like to share with you," said the AI therapist.

"I do?"

"Needs, remember?" coached N2ME-C.

Queen Crimson reclaimed the other items she hadn't taken with her to Tellusora. She slid her bejeweled knife into its hiding place in her boot and put her blaster in her pocket.

"Right, right. Listen, Mom, my need for choice isn't being met—"

"Insubordination! Your need for *breathing* won't be met soon. Report. Now, Prince Hunter."

Hunter glared at the sweet, plastic face of the AI therapist. "You see?"

"Mmm," N2ME-C said, prudently refraining from getting in the middle of this royal battle of wills.

"Did you bring back some fresh meat?" Prince Hunter asked his mother.

"What do I look like, Slobber Eats? It's high time you learned to hunt for yourself," Queen Crimson complained. "Did you enroll in the Assassin's Academy?"

"Er—well, no, but I found a great school. It's all online, so I wouldn't even have to leave home. I can learn how to make awesome VR and AR video games!"

"We don't have time to play *games*. We're fighting for our *survival*. And the survival of Rexhaven and Avenir. We can barely survive here under the Crowned Citadel. Haven't you listened to a single thing I've been telling you?" snapped Queen Crimson.

"Solar flares from our twin suns, toxic air, oxygen shortages, nuclear war, blah, blah, blah," Prince Hunter said drearily. "I heard you. But what can I do about it?"

Queen Crimson snorted. "You can enroll in the Assassin's Academy, for starters."

"I missed the deadline," Prince Hunter said petulantly.

"Deadline schmed-line. You're going, and that's that," Queen Crimson said imperiously.

Prince Hunter huffed resentfully.

"Prince Hunter is trying to tell you something, my queen," interceded N2ME-C.

"I've heard enough of his childish bellyaching." Queen Crimson drew up to her full, imposing height and glared at her son. She commanded, "Now report."

"Just one more school—what about the Multiverse Academy? That sounds far more interesting than the Assassin's Academy," said Prince Hunter.

"*Multiverse* Academy? On Tellusora? That can't be

—Opus Die has outlawed the very notion of the multiverse." Queen frowned, suddenly interested. "We can't have people suspecting their superiors come from off-world."

"Well, it must be secret then. The secret Multiverse Academy sounds like my kind of school."

"How did you hear about it?" Queen Crimson asked.

"It was a hushed conversation a raven sim overheard on Lokey—I mean, Tellusora."

"What could those chumps possibly know about the multiverse that we don't know?" Queen Crimson wondered.

"I could find out. They do know rather a lot about magic that we don't know."

"Our brand of magic is far more reliable—it's called technology," Queen Crimson said, affronted.

"How about I enroll in the secret Multiverse Academy? I could be your spy."

"Hmm. That does have some intriguing possibilities. But a bit difficult to pull off."

"Nothing you couldn't manage, I'm sure," Prince Hunter said, buttering up his mother.

"Hmm." Queen Crimson's look radiated superiority as she started scheming. She tented her fingers and tapped her forefingers together. "What else?"

"I downloaded the visual data—you know, from the raven sims—and guess what? I only caught a glimpse as it flashed past, but it appears that someone is using an old-fashioned car as a multiverse portal. One of those hydrogen-fueled cars with four rubber tires and no anti-grav propulsion."

"Ancient history—on Avenir. But Tellusora doesn't have cars yet. They're still using horses and carriages. So where in the multiverse could the intruders be from?"

"Dunno. But it seems that Opus Die has got competition colonizing Lok—Tellusora," said Prince Hunter.

"If the intruders are from somewhere else in the multiverse ... maybe we can mine *their* oxygen. Find that vehicle! It could be a portal key."

"I scanned already. Someone must have moved it."

"Scan again," Queen Crimson commanded.

Prince Hunter flexed his jaw and gritted his teeth, irritated by her imperious tone. He changed the topic and asked, "Are you going to tell Opus Die?"

"No, not yet. I've got to destroy the invaders first."

"Or at least apprehend them. Why are you always so bloodthirsty?"

"It's my nature. Yours, too. You'll see, now that you've finally reached puberty," said Queen Crimson.

"I'm not like you," said Prince Hunter.

"Then you'll die. Kill or be killed. Only the ruthless survive," Queen Crimson said.

"Is that true?" the AI therapist asked.

Queen Crimson picked up the remote and clicked it.

The AI therapist whirred, then stilled and became lifeless, proving Crimson's point.

"It is indisputable."

CHAPTER 25
IN THE CELLAR

BLUEBELLS INN, PROSPERUS, TELLUSORA.

The cavernous cold storage room was eerily silent.

Just the place to hide a dead body, thought Ana.

Light streaming through the open door illuminated sides of beef that hung from hooks in the ceiling, along with plucked chickens and long links of sausages. Enormous blocks of ice kept everything cold. The walls were flanked with shelves and crates of potatoes, cabbages, carrots, pickles, jam, and other items. The room smelled faintly of cabbage.

Ana, Zackary, Marilla and Veto paused on the threshold of the murky room.

And then … they heard a faint mewling sound.

Veto barked, "Cat! Cat! Cat!"

The mewling stopped.

"Bad dog!" Marilla scolded, then called her cat.

The room was quiet once again. Just as they were about to give up hope, the feeble mewling sound came again.

"There it is again!" Zackary whispered.

"Here, kitty-kitty-kitty!" Marilla coaxed.

"Do your animal charm thing, Ana Banana." Zackary nudged his sister.

"You're safe now. You can come out," Ana crooned. She softly sang "Ana's Song," and enveloped the space in calming energy. The tune stuck in her head, but she didn't know the words, so she sang, "La, la, la" to the tune of the soothing lullaby.

Marilla and Zackary relaxed, enchanted by the soothing song.

After a moment, the gray cat emerged from behind some wooden crates. The cat purred and rubbed against Ana. Four shivering newborn kittens trailed behind her, tumbling over each other.

"Kittens!" Marilla squealed, overjoyed. "Tom! Is that why you've been hiding?"

"Uh ... you need to rename your cat. He is a *she*," Zackary pointed out. "Definitely."

"I name you *Tammie,* Tommie!" Marilla laughed.

"Out! Out! All out!" Tammie meowed (but only Ana understood).

"Did you hear that?" Ana said.

"What?" Zackary rubbed his arms to keep warm, as he was shivering in the cold larder.

"The cat talked," said Ana.

Zackary rolled his eyes. "Give it a rest."

Marilla grabbed Tammie. Ana scooped up three shivering kittens. "Let's get into the warm."

Zackary grabbed the last kitten. "It's so cold in here. Why on Earth would a cat have her kittens here?"

"She must have gotten stuck in here." Ana cradled the three kittens in the skirt of her blue velvet dress. Veto followed.

Ana kicked the brick that held the door ajar and the heavy door swung shut. The latch caught with a loud click. They exited, leaving the frosty air behind, cheeks rosy from the chill air. Marilla raced to the kitchen, clutching her squirming cat.

In the kitchen, Marilla excitedly announced, "We found Tom! He's a *she!* I'm gonna call her Tammie. We found kittens, too! They were in the cold room!"

Rosalind gave Ana a grateful nod. "Cook was right. You're an animal charmer, and no mistake."

"It was a team effort," Ana said.

Purring, Tammie settled down to nurse her kittens in a basket by the fire. The little fur balls crowded around, nursing.

Marilla named the kittens. "You can be Whiskers. You can be Ginger. And you are ... Spot."

Shivering, Zackary stood by the fire to warm up.

"Where can we find the Wizard Snapdragon?" Ana asked Rosalind. They had to find a cure for her brother.

"I'll find out, like I promised. Mr. Berger is away on an errand for the Crimson Censor, but he should be back soon." Rosalind toyed anxiously with her apron. "I'll throw in a free meal. Lamb stew—one of my most popular dishes!"

Ana glanced at her pale brother, who shrugged. "And you'll ask him when he gets back?"

"Yes, although truth be told, I'm afraid to talk to him. He's so … so … so … I can't find the right word," Rosalind finished lamely.

"Rigid?" suggested Ana.

Rosalind flinched, eyes darting about nervously. "Shh!"

CHAPTER 26
PUPPET #2

The Bluebells Inn dining room was plain, practical, and unpretentious. The larger part of the dining room was outdoors. Benches flanked long wooden tables under the overhanging roof. Beyond that, in the pleasant garden surrounded by a wooden fence, more tables invited guests to linger over a pint or two and bask in the sunshine, or sit in the shade under the apple tree.

Zackary sketched a drawing of Egor, sticking his tongue in concentration. His version resembled Frankenstein.

Ana wrote in her journal, recording their multi-verse adventures. It was hard to capture the exact flavor of all the incredible things that had happened. But it was important, so she focused on her task with determination. Veto dozed at her feet.

She wrote, *When Zack is busy being creative, he's in a better mood.*

"What're you writing?"

"It's nothing." Ana covered the pages of her journal. As she did so, her sleeve pushed up, revealing a glint of burnished metal.

"Watch it!" Zackary warned. He tugged her sleeve over the bracelet.

Ana scanned the room and was relieved to see they were alone. "Thanks, Zee."

"I doubt our school newspaper—or any newspaper—will publish your story. No one will believe it."

"You sketch, I write." Ana closed her notebook. "It's our art. Publication is secondary."

"So, what's our plan, Ana Banana?"

"I have an idea." She insisted their mission should be to track down the Wizard Snapdragon. If the wizard healed Zackary, this whole adventure would be a gift! Then, hopefully, they could use the wardrobe portal to return to Earth.

Zackary argued that their priority should be to refuel the PUP. Egor had regaled him with stories of his ingenious scientific experiments; he could help. If they could separate water—H_2O, into H_2 and O, or hydrogen and oxygen, then they would be able to refuel the PUP and be on their way back to Earth.

Marilla entered the dining room through the open

patio doors, interrupting their hushed debate. Tammie stalked after her, tail held high, on a leash.

"Want an apple?" Marilla offered them the green apples she had gathered from the tree outside. Zackary took one.

"Friend!" Veto lunged toward the cat, but he was brought to an abrupt halt by his leash attached to the table leg.

The cat hissed and tried to flee. But her leash wrapped around Marilla's wrist prevented her from escaping. "Enemy!"

"Ow! Stop that!" Marilla loosened the leash, which was biting into her wrist.

"Come on, you two. Be nice," coaxed Ana.

"Friend! Let's play!" Veto wagged his tail.

"Keep away from me, you horrible brute," snarled the cat.

Zackary bit into a hard green apple and made a face. "Yuck! Sour!"

The kids stiffened as Mr. Berger entered, followed by three workers, each carrying a large rectangular item about the size of a man. Like Mr. Berger, the workers were wooden puppets, and they moved stiffly.

"Where do you want this, Mr. Berger?" asked a worker.

Mr. Berger pointed. "One there, another one over there. Put the third one here. Then everyone can enjoy them no matter where they're sitting. Chop-chop!"

The workers complied. They removed the protective blankets covering the large rectangular objects, revealing three large dark mirrors with silver frames.

Rosalind followed them in, huffing as she was short of breath. "What's this now?"

"Silver Screens. Gifts from the Crimson Censor," Mr. Berger said woodenly.

At the mention of the Crimson Censor, Ana flinched, knocking her pen off the table. She bent down to retrieve it.

"Mr. Berger, I'm wondering if you'd be so kind as to tell me where one could find the Wizard Snapdragon," Rosalind stammered.

"The traitor?"

"Traitor? Last week, you said how much you admired her—"

"Things have changed," growled Mr. Berger. "Now I know the Truth. Anyone associated with the Wizard Snapdragon is the enemy. We must destroy the enemy in the name of Opus Die, our God and protector."

Rosalind stepped back and held on to a wooden pillar to steady herself, her eyes wide with concern. She glanced up at Mr. Berger and saw the fire blazing in his eyes. "Thank you for telling me, Mr. Berger," she said in a servile voice, bowing her head.

Smart cook, thought Ana. *Talking to Mr. Berger is not safe. Not now.*

Crimson swept in to inspect the installation of the

Silver Screens. Her scarlet dress fluttered about her long legs and her stiletto heels clicked.

Zackary slouched behind a pillar, seemingly trying to become too insignificant to notice.

Ana quivered with fear, regretting that she had ever donned the mysterious cuffs. She knew she was doomed if the evil sorceress spotted them. But, if she stayed hidden beneath the table, she might yet save herself and Zackary. Egor said the cuffs were imperative, but she didn't know how to harness their power. Were they more trouble than they were worth?

"Adequate, Mr. Berger, adequate." This was high praise coming from Crimson, who was miserly with compliments.

"I'm crooked," complained the mirror nearest Ana.

Ana froze in shock.

Crimson strode toward the mirror, intent on straightening it. In a minute, she'd spot Ana!

Belatedly, Ana realized she had left her journal on the table. If Crimson so much as glanced it, it would be a catastrophe. And if Crimson read it, everything and everyone she loved would be in jeopardy. Ana was used to keeping secrets, but she spilled everything on the page. She wrote to untangle her most intimate thoughts and feelings. Her journal was the place where she tried to make sense of the mystery of her family and the multiverse.

Terrified, Ana scuttled farther under the table. It

was a lousy hiding place. Needing a distraction, Ana freed Veto from his leash. "Go, boy!" she whispered, unsure if the dog would listen or stay by her side.

"Yes, master—Ana," said Veto, delighted to help.

Veto bounded toward the cat, which fled, yanking her leash out of Marilla's hands. "Ow!"

The cat bolted, and Veto eagerly gave chase. The animals raced past Crimson, tripping her. Crimson stumbled in a most undignified—and hilarious—manner.

Furious, Crimson muttered something under her breath and clinked her cuffs together. The metal reverberated like a gong.

The cat shimmered and transformed into a wooden puppet.

Marilla gasped, her mouth a wide O of surprise. She blinked back tears at the sight of her cat. Tammie howled.

Veto scurried out the open doors into the garden, ran past the apple trees, and vanished.

"Resistance is futile." Crimson stormed out after the little dog.

Ana exhaled with relief from her hiding place on the floor out of sight. She risked easing her journal off the table and into her pocket.

Marilla's lower lip wobbled. She grabbed Tammie, who clattered, no longer a soft, warm, cuddly cat.

Eyes brimming with tears, she gazed imploringly

at her father. "Daddy, she turned my cat into a puppet!"

"Stop whining and sniveling," said her father.

Rosalind gasped in shock, as he was normally such a doting father. The Crimson Censor had changed more than his exterior.

"Chop-chop!" Mr. Berger left.

Marilla burst into tears.

CHAPTER 27
A MAGICAL MISTAKE

In the Bluebells Inn kitchen, Ana, Zackary, and Marilla tried to feed the newborn kittens.

The kittens cried anxiously and tumbled blindly over each other, trying to nurse. They pawed at their mother, but Tammie didn't produce any nourishing milk.

Ana realized that the wooden cat would not feed the hungry kittens or give them any comfort when they tried to snuggle against her hard body.

Marilla placed a saucer of milk near the kittens, but they had never drunk from a saucer before and they didn't seem interested. She pushed a kitten's nose into the saucer of warm milk. It resisted and sneezed. Tiny droplets of milk splattered, and the kitten looked ridiculous, with white droplets all over its whiskers and ears. But it licked its fur and got its first taste of the milk.

Marilla laughed. "Your name can be Clown. 'Cause you're a silly little kitten."

Veto wanted to drink milk from the saucer, but Ana pushed him away. "That's not for you, Veto. That's for the kittens."

With his nose, Veto pushed the kittens toward the saucer of milk. Ana snapped a photo.

"They're goners, just like me," Zackary said.

"You mustn't think like that," Ana scolded.

"They're all gonna die without their mother," Zackary said.

Ana felt a lump in her throat as she thought, *We didn't die without our mother. But we struggled.*

"Don't let my kittens die! Please ... do something!" Marilla said.

"I have an idea, Marilla. But I need your help. I need to borrow your keys," said Ana.

"Why?"

"We animal whisperers are sworn to protect all living creatures. That includes you and your cat ... and these four cute fur balls."

Marilla withdrew the silver chain concealed under her dress. Upon it hung two keys, one large, one small. She hesitated. "My dad told me to never give these keys to anyone."

"I'm not anyone. I'm your friend."

Marilla toyed with the keys, hesitating. "What're you gonna do?"

"See if I can reverse the spell and bring your cat back to life."

"And my dad?" Marilla asked, her voice cracking.

"And your dad," agreed Ana.

"You promise to bring them back?"

"I promise to do my very best," Ana said courageously. "Trust me."

Marilla handed Ana the silver chain with the two master keys.

"Thanks. Now, we need to feed these little darlings. There's got to be a dropper or turkey baster somewhere in this kitchen," Ana said.

"I'll search the pantry." Marilla skipped into the spacious pantry.

"Stay here with Marilla, Zackary. Try to get the kittens to drink milk."

"Where do you think you're going, Ana Banana?"

"I have a hunch. What if the secret to restoring Mr. Berger and Tammie is in that wardrobe? I saw the Crimson Censor walk into it—like it was a portal. I have to check that wardrobe."

"What if the secret is those bracelets?" Zackary pointed to the magical cuffs adorning Ana's wrists. "What if they can reverse the spell? Let's try that first."

"Good idea," agreed Ana. "What shall I try it on?"

"The wooden cat. Obviously."

"But what if I make things worse?" Ana worried.

"How much worse can it get?"

"Good point."

Zackary placed the wooden cat on the floor, away from the basket of kittens. Veto watched curiously. He cocked his head to one side.

Ana tapped her gleaming cuffs together, and they made a reverberating ringing vibration. The air shimmered. Veto barked. But Tammie remained unchanged—still a wooden cat.

"Try again," Zackary urged. "Maybe you have to say something."

Marilla fearfully peered out from the pantry. "What's that noise? What are you doing?"

"We're trying to make things better," Zackary said. "Go on now. It's not safe out here. Shut the door, Marilla."

Marilla retreated into the pantry, shutting the door behind her.

Ana tried again. She focused on the wooden cat puppet, clanged the metal cuffs together and proclaimed, "Transform now!"

As she said these words, a kitten scampered in the way and got caught unexpectedly in the crossfire. Clown shimmered and turned into a wooden puppet. Tammie remained unchanged.

"Oh, no!" Ana was horrified by what she had done.

Now there were two wooden puppets on the floor: one cat ... and one kitten.

"Try again! Maybe you can reverse it," urged Zackary.

Ana nodded grimly. She concentrated on the wooden kitten and clanged the cuffs together. This time, she said the words with conviction laced with desperation. "Transform now! Back to life!"

The kitten shimmered and transformed from wood into living fur, flesh, and blood. Clown meowed and shook himself vigorously.

The magic took Ana's breath away. But Tammie remained as wooden as ever.

"We're back where we started. It's hopeless," Zackary said glumly. "You okay?"

"I'm absolutely fine," Ana lied. "But I can't reverse Crimson's spells."

"Mmm. But it seems that you *can* make your own spells and reverse them."

"What good is that? I don't want to turn anyone into wood." Ana shivered as her imagination plagued her with dire consequences. But all she said was, "I wish I knew how to use these."

"Better not use them. They're likely to backfire," warned Zackary. "What if you turn *yourself* into a totem pole?"

Ana set her jaw resolutely. "I *have to* check out the wardrobe in the Censor's room. There has got to be some clue that will help us revive Tammie and Mr. Berger."

"No way. It's too dangerous!" His eyes became white and wild again, and it seemed he would explode.

Fortunately, Ana knew what to do. "Zackary, what's the most common hydrogen vehicle?"

"The forklift," Zackary said, shifting rapidly from outrage into his calm lecturer mode. "As the only exhaust from hydrogen-powered forklifts is water, they are ideal for enclosed spaces like warehouses. Also, they are much quicker to refuel than electric forklifts, so that saves time and labor costs. Most people don't know that recharging a hydrogen-fueled vehicle takes minutes, whereas recharging an electric vehicle can take hours. Hydrogen-powered cars could be the next wave of green energy. Toyota, Honda, and Hyundai all have commercially available models, but my personal favorite is the …"

Ana zoned out until he'd exhausted his expertise, which took some time. When Zackary stopped talking, she said, "You're quite the expert, Zackary."

Zackary grinned. "True. You like animals, I like machines."

Ana took some cookies from the cookie jar, gave a couple to Zackary, and put the rest in her pocket. "Eat something. I think you've got low blood sugar."

Zackary munched on a cookie, and color returned

to his pale face. He pushed away a wispy lock of hair.

"Please, Ana. I'm a good boy." Veto begged for a cookie. Ana fed him a morsel, and he wagged his curly tail, which waved over his back.

"I need you to stay with Marilla," Ana told her brother.

"No way, I'm coming with you," Zackary said stubbornly. "Courage is a muscle and all that. You need backup."

Ana hesitated. She didn't want to mention that her brother was still weak and vulnerable. She wanted him to think of himself as strong and healthy, because he would become whatever he focused on.

Ana chose her words carefully. "I do need backup. You're right about that. But one of us needs to stay with Marilla. She lost her father and her cat. We can't abandon her now. The other one can explore. I have the golden cuffs. And Marilla likes you."

"I don't know about that."

"I should go. You should stay."

Zackary hesitated, but her logic was sound. "Hmm."

"I'll be back in fifteen minutes," Ana promised.

"And if you're not?" Zackary fretted.

"Don't be such a worrywart. I'll be absolutely fine."

"Can I come out now?" Marilla peered out from the pantry.

"One minute, Marilla."

"What if you get turned into wood?" Zackary asked, worried.

"I won't," Ana said with false bravado. "What if I learn how to turn wooden people—and pets—back into flesh and blood? We have to do something!"

"Okay." Zackary relented. "But be back in twenty. No more."

"Deal," agreed Ana.

"It's safe now, Marilla," Zackary called. Marilla came out of the pantry, and he gave her one of the cookies. "Did you find a dropper to feed the kittens?"

"Not yet." Marilla pawed through a kitchen drawer filled with utensils.

Ana eased toward the door. Veto trotted after her.

"Could we use this?" Marilla showed a turkey baster to Zackary.

"Let's try it," Zackary said.

Veto tried to follow Ana out of the kitchen. "I'm coming."

"Stay!" Ana told him firmly.

"Take me! I'm your lie detector and secret protector!"

"Stay. Protect Zackary and Marilla," said Ana.

"Take me! You need me!" insisted Veto.

But Ana slipped out of the kitchen alone.

Veto slumped onto the floor and put his forlorn face between his paws. "Mistake."

CHAPTER 28
ROOM #33

Ana crept softly up the stairs, her heart pounding in her chest. She checked the corridor and saw a maid. She ducked back into the stairway and waited until the maid entered a room with her cleaning supplies.

Once the coast was clear, Ana crept down the hallway toward number 33, the Crimson Censor's room. Clenched tightly in her hands, so it wouldn't jingle, was the chain that held Marilla's two master keys.

Glancing around to ensure she was alone, she tried the doorknob, but the door was locked. Ana tried a key in the lock, but it wouldn't go in.

She inhaled sharply. A quick glance up and down the hallway revealed no one. She had to hurry!

Ana flipped the key with shaking hands and tried again. This time, the key slid in easily.

Ana opened the door and the sight of a grandly appointed chamber greeted her. The hotel room contained a four-poster bed, a once-luxurious but now-faded carpet, and the object of her desire—the wardrobe. Ana slipped into the room, quietly closing the door behind her.

"Resistance is futile!" challenged a husky voice.

Terror shot through Ana as she whirled to confront the Crimson Censor—but it was only the parrot. Ana laughed shakily.

"Oh, it's only you. I nearly jumped right out of my skin!" With trembling hands, she put the chain with the master keys around her neck, then padded toward the parrot. "Hello, my pretty."

The parrot cocked its head, peering at her through the bars of its gilded cage with one bright eye. It was a magnificent bird, unlike any Ana had ever seen. Nearly as large as a swan, the pretty parrot was covered in red feathers that transitioned to yellow and then blue at the wing tips.

In a voice that mocked Crimson's husky alto, the bird squawked, "If I want your opinion, I'll tell it to you."

"What silly nonsense. If you told it to me, it wouldn't be my opinion then, would it?" Ana took a cookie from her pocket, broke off a piece, and offered the treat to the parrot. "Polly, want a cracker?"

"If I want your opinion, I'll tell it to you." The bird gobbled the treat.

Ana hesitated, torn between the parrot and the wardrobe. The wardrobe won. The tall armoire was a thing of beauty, inlaid with contrasting light and dark wood.

"Why would anyone walk *into* this wardrobe?" Ana said conversationally to the parrot. "Is it a portal?"

Surely her aunt and uncle and father would be worried about her. Well, maybe not her father. When he was on a shoot, he had no time for her. But now was not the time to ruminate about that.

Focus, Ana. Focus!

Ana tried to open the wardrobe door, but it was locked. She tried one key, but it was too big. Then she tried the tiny key, and it slid in. The wardrobe opened with a click.

Ana swung the door open eagerly, but slumped, disillusioned, as there was nothing inside but fine clothes. She touched the back of the wardrobe and discovered wood. She tapped on the boards softly to make sure, and they sounded ordinary. Her fingers searched along the frame, seeking a latch, but found nothing. If the wardrobe held a hidden doorway, she couldn't find it. She must have missed something—but what?

Ana remembered one of her favorite books, *The Lion, the Witch and the Wardrobe.* In that book, the wardrobe had been full of fur coats and moth balls. But this wardrobe held breathtaking garments made of astonishing materials, including an iridescent ball gown, a chain-mail vest as light as paper, and stern scarlet jackets designed to command respect—and possibly outright surrender.

It was like the wardrobe department on a movie set, where you could become any character simply with a change of clothes. Ana ran her fingers over the fine fabrics, lingering over several incredible outfits, making up stories about the kind of character she'd be in each costume. Finally, she selected a magnificent blue cashmere cloak and slipped it on. The cloak was too large, but the color complemented her blue dress perfectly. She felt formidable like Wonder Woman with the sweeping cape-like cloak and her burnished cuffs.

Ana spun in front of the mirror mounted on the inside of the wardrobe door and admired her reflection as she twirled. Suddenly, a rattle at the door jolted Ana out of her trance.

"Oh, no!" Ana leaped into the wardrobe and pulled the door shut behind her—but not completely, as she didn't want to get stuck inside.

Through the crack, Ana glimpsed the Crimson Censor enter the room. She heard the clatter of footsteps against the plank floor, then the rustle of fabric as Crimson took off her red jacket.

Uh-oh. Would she hang her jacket in the wardrobe and discover Ana? Ana shrank backward, but there was nowhere to hide, and she dared not move her feet. She held her breath.

Crimson tossed her jacket and hat on the bed. Ana felt a surge of relief and exhaled softly.

"Mommy's home," Crimson crooned as she opened the door to the parrot's cage. She wore a regal red dress that showed off her tiny waist and flared to wide, studded shoulders.

She snapped her fingers twice, and the parrot responded to this command by climbing onto her padded shoulders. Crimson commanded, "Apertus!

And then strangest thing happened. The air crackled and smelled sharp, like ozone or chlorine. The gowns in the closet shimmered, blurred, and vanished.

Reality realigned, colors spinning like a kaleidoscope.

CHAPTER 29
THE PORTAL

CROWNED CITADEL, REXHAVEN, AVENIR.

The wardrobe *was* a portal! But what had made it open?

Frost crunched underfoot as Ana entered the cold, strange world. The alpine tundra was stiff with permafrost. She shivered but marched on as this parallel universe held the answers she needed. Dwarf shrubs stood like menacing sentries in the mist. Lichen-covered boulders resembled threatening hunchbacks about to surge out of the mist and attack her.

"Gotcha!" Ana heard, and she startled. But it was only her imagination run amuck and a crow, invisible in the distance, cawing from an unseen perch.

Stop that negative thinking, she told herself in no

uncertain terms. Then, before her monkey mind flooded her with chatter about all the things that could go wrong, would go wrong, or might go wrong, she drowned it out. In her imagination, she landed a role in the new *Star Trek* series, the opportunity of a lifetime for an aspiring actress like her. She resolved to give a stellar performance. *My mission is: "to explore strange new worlds, to seek out new life and new civilizations, to boldly go where no one has gone before."*

As she took a few bold steps into the strange world, she struggled to catch her breath. The air smelled foul. She gasped for air, trying to fill her lungs, but the air was so thin she became dizzy and lightheaded from lack of oxygen.

Her nose started to run. Without thinking, she wiped her nose with her sleeve. Blood smeared on the sleeve of the beautiful blue cloak. Her heart sank. The cloak was ruined. Bloodstains were impossible to remove, as everyone knew. She groaned in frustration.

If she'd been Lucy in Narnia, she would have had a lace handkerchief in her pocket. She had neither a handkerchief nor a tissue. She held her finger under the trickle of blood dripping from her nose.

Taking her asthma puffer out of her pocket, she inhaled a dose of medicine. It helped her breathe but didn't do a thing to stop her nosebleed.

She glanced at the sleeve and was astonished to

see the bloodstain fading. Mesmerized, she watched the dark crimson stain gradually vanish until it was completely gone. She inspected the fabric—it was perfect, just as if it were brand new.

"A self-cleaning coat. Cool!" Ana murmured, encouraged by this minor miracle.

Her nosebleed had stopped, and her breathing had improved, so she set off again. She shivered in the cold and wished she had a scarf, hat, and mittens. And tissues. The winter weather was a sharp contrast to the hot summer weather in Tellusora. She stuffed her icy hands into her pockets.

Where on Earth—or off Earth—was she?

Ana quivered as she slowly advanced into the unknown. Overhead, a gigantic white dome spanned the sky. She glimpsed a mansion in the distance and realized the dome was sheltering about a dozen acres, including the tract of land from the portal to the mansion. It reminded Ana of the iconic, translucent roof of B. C. Place Stadium, which hosted concerts and football matches.

She put her asthma puffer back in her pocket and her fingers grazed her phone. She took it out and snapped a few photos so she could show Zackary the clever machinery of the dome ceiling. He'd like that.

The air was thin, cold, and barely life-sustaining. Clutching the cloak close over her nose, she hoped it would filter through the foul-smelling air. Each plodding step felt like scaling a mountain peak, and her breath came in feeble gasps. Ana remembered tales of Mount Everest and the death zone, where brave adventurers were forced to turn back or succumb to suffocation from lack of oxygen.

Fear coursed through her veins as she fought for each shallow breath. On the verge of a panic attack, she remembered all the times she couldn't breathe and had to be rushed to the hospital in an ambulance, sirens wailing.

If that happens now, I'll die. Not helpful, she chided her imagination. *Stop that. If you're going to be like that, I won't listen to you. I am capable and competent, and I can handle this! I am capable and competent, and I can handle this!*

As she fought to control her ragged breathing, she felt a surprising surge of empathy for her brother and his Zack attacks. *Maybe we're not so different, after all.*

Ana trekked along the curved wall at the base of the dome until she reached a window that revealed the landscape beyond the protective dome. She gasped in consternation at the scene of ruin.

Orange and gray air swirled with toxic fumes. Blackened shrubs scratched the sky with gnarled fingers. A thin veil of snow covered the ground. Twin suns blazed cheerlessly in a bruised sky. Ana didn't see a single living thing, not even a blade of grass or an insect. The place felt evil.

What great catastrophe occurred here? Who lives in that mansion? What does this strange world have to do with people and cats being turned to wood?

She pushed on, knowing that many lives depended upon her, resolutely determined to find answers.

CHAPTER 30
THE GHASTLY GARDEN

As she trudged toward the mansion in the mist, Ana discovered a stone wall which encircled a frost-covered garden. Exploring it, Ana discovered a frozen fountain adorned with with graceful nymphs with dead leaves welded into the ice. Evergreen bushes had once been trimmed into neat hedges, but now they stood askew, weighed down by ice. Once, someone had cared for this garden, but now it was abandoned. Nothing grew here.

A beautiful marble statue of a winged angel towered over a half dozen smaller statues, as if guarding them. While the statues were amazingly life-like, they didn't inspire her with their craftsmanship. They made her uneasy. Upon closer inspection, she discovered that the life-sized statues were not made of marble or bronze, but of some strange material covered with ice and frost.

One statue seemed eerily familiar. It resembled the porter who had taken the Crimson Censor's luggage to her room. He wore a shocked expression, his mouth agape, and his eyes wide with fear. It gave her the creeps. Who'd put that statue in their garden? It was ghastly. And ... could it actually *be* that porter? The hairs stood up on the nape of her neck.

Out of the corner of her eye, Ana glimpsed something moving. Hold on—hadn't that marble angel been farther away? Had it moved closer? She scurried off, anxious to get away from the garden's creepy statues. They made her think of the uncanny valley.

Something rumbled and clanked. Ana stalked toward the racket and discovered a machine the size of a large truck, blazoned with the brand *Clean Air* in cheerful sky-blue letters. She hadn't seen it earlier, as it had been obscured by the rock wall around the garden. Whirring and pumping, it sounded like a great, breathing beast. The sleek machine had light-emitting digital readouts that displayed ever-changing numbers. A small white plastic plate on the chassis discreetly announced the model in black letters: *Clean Air Beta 11-B*.

Touching a readout, Ana wondered aloud, "What's this?" In the icy chill of the frigid air, her words formed a small puff of fog as she spoke.

She jumped in surprise when someone answered, "Oxygen intake valve. Currently, mining twenty-five percent oxygen in excellent range. Do you want more information?"

Ana spun around anxiously, her heart pounding in her chest as she searched for a sign of life. The palatial mansion loomed even larger and darker in the distance. No grotesque stone figure had followed her from the garden. The stunted shrubs stood like ominous sentries, shrouded in fog. She realized it was the machine that had answered her question.

Ana was grateful for the Babbler-eels in her ears. The universal translators were extremely handy for anyone traveling across the multiverse.

"More information. Yes. Please." Ana wasn't sure if you needed to say please to a machine, but good manners were always a good idea. And anyway, they were a habit her father had drilled into her.

The machine responded, "Today's harvest: fourteen tons of air. Oxygen at 22.18% volume, carbon dioxide 250 parts per million. Trace elements of hydrogen, helium, crypton, xenon, and iodine recovered for reprocessing. Today's air quality interior dome maintained at 17.18% oxygen, carbon dioxide 450 parts per million: acceptable. Exterior dome air quality: 12.26% oxygen: toxic, acid rain, hostile to all life forms. Do you want more information?" It ended cheerfully with the company slogan. "Clean Air keeps you breathing!"

"How about the roof?"

"Roof status update: pneumatically stabilized membrane cushions of triple-skinned fabric are resisting the corrosive atmosphere as expected. Replacement recommended in 221 cycles. The steel masts and steel cables have a half-life of 931 cycles." Once again, the machine ended brightly. "Clean Air keeps you breathing!"

Ana realized it was an air-mining machine. The equipment sucked air into the dome with a steady mechanical pump.

But where is the good air coming from?

The enormous pipe plunged through the dome wall, then vanished into a fog-covered mirror. Beyond that, she could see nothing through the dense fog bank.

"Where do these pipes go?"

"Off world," the Clean Air machine replied.

Not helpful. Ana knocked on the massive pipe. "What's this?"

"Air intake pipe. Do you want more information?"

"More information, yes, please."

"Mine site 2A report: oxygen at 23.18% today, down from 24.97%. Clean Air keeps you breathing!"

Ana suddenly realized what was happening. "You're stealing air!"

"Mining air," corrected the machine. "See license 25-E-38913 for authorization to exploit natural resources from Lokey, the region the inhabitants call Verdant, Tellusora."

"You can't do that!"

"Clean Air keeps you breathing!" The Clean Air machine cheerfully repeated.

No wonder Rosalind was short of breath and Marilla was turning blue from asthma attacks! Someone was literally sucking the air from the room. No, not the room—sucking the air from another world.

This diabolical evil is on a planetary scale. Can I stop it? Can anyone?

CHAPTER 31
ILLEGAL ALIEN

In the distance, Ana glimpsed a massive structure under construction outside the protective dome. It resembled a gigantic Clean Air machine. Huge black pipes extended like octopus arms from the ominous structure. She felt troubled. "What is that?"

"What's what?" said the Clean Air machine.

"What's that?" Ana pointed, then realized the machine couldn't see her finger pointing. "That half-built structure over there with the big pipes sticking out of it. It looks like a gigantic air-mining machine. Am I right?"

"Insufficient data," the Clean Air machine said. "Clean Air keeps you breathing!"

Suddenly, two robots came around the side of the Clean Air machine and surrounded Ana menacingly.

One robot was small, with a label on the side that read *Customs*. The other was large and intimidating, stiffly erect, and reminded Ana of a soldier. The Military Robot loomed menacingly, while the smaller Customs Robot spoke in official gobbledygook.

"Welcome to Avenir," droned the Customs Robot, not sounding welcoming in the least. One metal finger hovered over a touchscreen pad, poised to take down incriminating data.

"Oh! You surprised me," Ana said, startled.

"Initiating customs protocol. Purpose of visit? Business or pleasure?" the Customs Robot asked.

"What?" stammered Ana.

"Business or pleasure?"

"Uh ... pleasure, I guess. Trip Advisor suggested a jaunt to visit the Hampton Court Palace, but I seem to have taken a wrong turn somewhere. Can you direct me to Hampton Court Palace?"

"You are confused. The only palace here is the Crowned Citadel, and Queen Cacophony never receives unscheduled visitors. Nationality?" asked the Customs Robot.

"Oh—I see. I'll just be on my way, sorry to have troubled you." Ana's breath came out in puffs in the chilly air. "You know how unreliable Google maps can be at times."

She started to back away, but her retreat was blocked by the massive Military Robot.

"Nationality?" insisted the Customs Robot.

"I'm from Los Angeles, California. I'm American."

"American," the Customs Robot repeated with metallic disdain. It punched the data into the electronic notepad with a mechanical finger. "That's not a registered Avenir nationality. No locals discount. Alien rate applicable. Submit payment for air tax."

"Air tax? What? Air is free." Ana's brow furrowed.

"No unauthorized person or persons may inhale oxygen without paying for it. Arid, Avenir, regulation #A-19-702-1314. Submit payment now."

Ana felt trapped, but she couldn't see a way to escape. The Clean Air machine blocked her way on one side, and the two robots hemmed her in on the other side. The once-lovely garden with the eery statues and frozen fountain was the nearest cover, not counting the bulk of the nearby Clean Air machine. The wardrobe portal she had entered through was far away.

A glowing digital readout showed the total amount due.

"Pay seventy-one Avenir dollars. Scan chip," insisted the Customs Robot. It held a scanning device near Ana's forehead. The device whirred. "Facial scan incomplete, no matching data in memory banks. No digital ID, no Avenir bank account," the Customs Robot accused.

"Uh … I'll be on my way." Ana edged away, but the Military Robot blocked her path.

"Submit payment," insisted the Customs Robot.

"Do you accept Apple pay?"

"Negative."

The beaded bracelet Marilla had given Ana still encircled her thumb. She offered it to the Customs Robot. "How about this?"

"Worthless junk," rumbled the Customs Robot.

As Ana had the audacity to continue breathing, the air tax continued to grow. The glowing digits kept increasing on the device. She thrust the childish bracelet into her pocket.

The Customs Robot droned, "You owe seventy-three Avenir dollars … seventy-four … seventy-five. Cease breathing immediately if you cannot pay the air tax!"

"I can't stop breathing!" Ana protested. "Don't be ridiculous!"

"Stop breathing right now!" The Customs Robot sounded a shrill alarm. "Thief. Stealing oxygen." Whirling red lights flashed on its head. "Illegal alien. Unauthorized access. Detain! Detain! Detain!"

Ana ran.

The tall Military Robot rapidly extended a long, telescoping mechanical arm and grabbed her. She tried to wriggle away, but she was no match for the massive Military Robot. It held her firmly.

"Let me go! Let me go!" Ana writhed, trying to escape. In the struggle, her long sleeves slid up, revealing a glint of something metal encircling her wrists.

Then something miraculous happened. The cuffs blasted a bolt of electric energy, which surged around the Military Robot. For a moment, it wreathed him in light. The electrical blast fried his circuits and blew his fuses. He dropped Ana and jerked oddly, then froze. His next stop would be the repair shop—or the junkyard.

The short Customs Robot reached for Ana, suddenly extending sharp screwdrivers where a human hand would have fingernails. It reminded Ana of *Edward Scissorhands*. The pointed tips scraped her arm, drawing blood. Ana kicked away the Customs Robot. Determined to escape, she scrambled to her feet and fled, the blue cloak fluttering behind her.

Ana ran abruptly into a woman who towered over her.

"Crimson!" gasped Ana, realizing that the Scarlet sorceress must have entered through the wardrobe portal, her footsteps masked by all the commotion. Ana stumbled backward, but Crimson held her shoulders in a vise-like grip.

"You stole my cloak," Crimson observed. A cruel smile playing on her scarlet lips marred her icy beauty. She was dressed warmly in a black-and-white Cossack fox-fur hat trimmed with crimson feathers, and a luxurious fox-fur coat trimmed with scarlet.

"Borrowed!"

"If I want your opinion, I'll tell it to you," squawked the parrot perched on Crimson's shoulder, its colorful red, yellow, and blue plumage contrasting with her creamy skin.

Crimson saw the smoking, ruined Military Robot and narrowed her eyes. "How on Avenir did you—" She grabbed Ana's wrist and yanked it, revealing the Emerald Censor's golden cuff.

"Ow! Lemme go!"

"It was *you!* You killed Emerald. You stole her cuffs."

"I don't know what you're talking about. I bought these at Nordstrom," Ana lied.

Crimson wrenched Ana's arm close to her face, as if to inspect the cuffs. But then she surprised Ana. Her tongue flashed out past her scarlet lips and licked the blood trickling from Ana's scraped arm. Her forked tongue was cold, and Ana shuddered with revulsion.

"Resistance is futile!" squawked the parrot.

"Lemme go!" Ana struggled wildly to escape, but Crimson held her, inhumanly strong.

"You killed a Censor," snarled Crimson. "So you must die, brat."

CHAPTER 32
RUN, ANA, RUN!

"Let my sister go!" Zackary yelled as he ran toward Ana and Crimson, surprising them both. He had emerged from behind the stone wall encircling the garden. He raced toward them, dodging boulders, his footsteps crunching over the frozen ground.

He was having a Zack attack. His explosive rage was exactly the right manic, unstoppable energy to rescue his sister. Zackary was so intense he seemed otherworldly, like a demigod.

"Leave her alone, you wicked witch!" Zackary hurled several hard, green apples at Crimson.

Crimson ducked, and the apples whizzed by her. The parrot flew off her shoulder, rocking her balance.

"If I want your opinion, I'll tell it to you!" squawked the parrot.

He grabbed another handful of green missiles from the basket—Marilla's basket—strapped across his shoulder. Ana fought to wrench her arm free, but Crimson kept her tight, icy grip clamped on Ana's wrist.

Veto raced toward Ana, barking furiously. He nipped at Crimson's ankles. "Let her go, you bloody predator!"

"Miserable rat! Get off!" Crimson kicked at the lapdog, but missed. She lost her balance, tripped, and fell. She was forced to let go of Ana.

"Bad person! Bad!" Veto lunged at Crimson's beautiful face, teeth bared. He was quite ferocious for a little dog, especially when his intended victim was on the ground. Crimson scrambled to get away from his teeth.

"Run, Ana, run!" Zackary yelled. "Go back!"

"Come on, Zackary, Veto!"

Ana fled toward the wardrobe portal. It seemed she might make it to safety.

Crimson snarled at Veto, showing her unnaturally long, sharp, white incisors. Tables turned, the little dog cowered. Crimson arose and kicked Veto. The kick landed, hard. Veto yelped and went flying.

Crimson clapped her cryptic cuffs, and they echoed with a ringing sound. She muttered something and pointed the ball of energy at Ana's fleeing back.

The energy shot toward Ana and encircled her—

but it bounced off her into a nearby bush. The bush sparkled and shattered into fragments of ice.

"Opus Die!" Crimson swore in frustration.

Crimson did it again, smacking her cuffs together with a metallic ringing sound, then blasting the ball of light at Ana. The energy shot—but once again, the energy bounced off. A nearby tree shimmered and turned to ice.

"Those blasted cuffs!" Crimson swore.

The golden cuffs protected Ana. But they didn't protect anyone else.

Crimson cracked her burnished cuffs together again. The sound rang out. This time, she pointed the ball of energy at Zackary.

"Duck, Zack!" Ana cried.

The shot crackled through the air like lightning. Zackary dodged it. The lightning bolt narrowly missed Marilla, who shrieked, her eyes wide with fear. For the first time, Ana noticed that the little girl had followed Zackary into Avenir. *Oh no!*

"Go home, Marilla!" Zackary yelled. "I told you *not* to follow me."

Rooted to the spot, Marilla's body trembled like a leaf in a storm as she clung to Tammie. But the wooden cat could not provide any protection.

Ana neared the wardrobe portal. A few more steps and she would be safe. Torn for a microsecond between cowardice and courage, she bolstered her resolve by embracing her imaginary role as a brave, loyal Star Fleet officer. She did the heroic thing and sprinted back toward Marilla, determined to save the child.

Crimson smacked her bright cuffs together with a menacing crack that echoed a warning throughout the tundra. She pointed the glowing ball of energy directly at Zackary with a calculating smirk. Undeterred by her formidable display, Veto barked and nipped at Crimson's ankles, throwing off her aim just enough for Zackary to dodge the attack once again.

The electrical energy cut through the air and struck a nearby bush, which froze and then shattered into thousands of shards in the wind.

Ana grabbed Marilla's small sticky hand and shoved her towards the portal with all her might. "Run home now, Marilla!"

Marilla took off like lightning, stumbling over herself in her haste to reach safety.

Ana pivoted fiercely to face Crimson, her own burnished cuffs clashing together with a deafening sound. A sizzling ball of energy began to grow around her hands, crackling and pulsating like a storm cloud. With a bellowing cry, she hurled the charge at Crimson, who deftly raised her cuffs in defense. The energy erupted harmlessly on contact, ricocheting off of Crimson's barrier and striking Veto.

Veto yelped. He was propelled backward by the

force of the blast before freezing solid like an ice sculpture. Aghast, Ana's eyes widened and locked onto the frozen form of her beloved companion.

Crimson fired again, arcs of electricity lancing out towards Marilla as she fled towards the wardrobe portal. The lightning struck with explosive power, wreathing Marilla in iridescent light as she was flung backwards against a rock wall. In seconds, she too had become a lifeless statue of a little girl clutching a cat puppet in utter terror. Ana gasped in horror.

Can I reverse the spell? I have to!

With a desperate cry, Ana smashed her cuffs together. An orb of lightning emanated from her hands, crackling and seething with energy as it raced toward Marilla.

Ana pleaded, "Reverse the spell! Bring her back to life!"

But the powerful bolt of magic careened off Marilla's still body and ricocheted away uselessly.

"Get out of here, Ana! You can't save her!" Zackary yelled, throwing green apples at Crimson and dodging her fire.

But Ana tried again, smacking her cuffs together again, unleashing an even more intense ball of energy that she sent toward the helpless little girl.

"Reverse the spell! Back to life!" Ana commanded.

Once again, light encircled Marilla, but the little girl remained frozen. As the spell cast toward Marilla bounced wildly off, it hit Veto, miraculously reviving him. The little dog transformed from an ice statue back to life.

Veto scrambled toward Ana, barking madly, "Let's get out of here!"

"Veto!" Ana cried out in shock and joy, barely able to take in his miraculous transformation.

Changing tactics, Crimson yanked a menacing blaster from her pocket, aiming it at Ana.

"I'll get you!" she spat viciously, marching forward.

"Resistance is futile!" screeched the parrot.

"She's got a gun!" Zackary yelled, his voice reverberating as Crimson advanced on his sister. "I'm dead either way. But you—you've got to live. For *both* of us. Run, Ana, run for your life!"

CHAPTER 33
A NOBLE SACRIFICE

"No! Don't, Zee!" Ana protested, but her brother ignored her.

"Run, Ana Banana!" Zackary shouted, his eyes white and wild, in the grip of another Zack attack.

Heedless of his own safety, Zackary hurled himself at the Scarlet sorceress, yelling like an enraged madman.

Crimson pointed her blaster at Ana, but Zackary deliberately blocked her shot, putting himself in the line of fire so his sister could escape. He bravely dodged and weaved, narrowly eluding Crimson's fire.

As he ran, Zackary hurled apples at Crimson. She ducked one hard green apple, then another. But the third apple smacked her in the mouth.

"Ow!" Crimson touched her bleeding lip. The red

blood trickling into her mouth contrasted with her bright white teeth and unnaturally long, sharp incisors. "You're gonna pay for that!"

Intent upon revenge, Crimson smacked her cuffs together and shot a blast of energy at Zackary. Lightning crackled through the air.

"No!" Ana watched as her brother was thrown backward against a stone wall. He morphed into a frozen statue.

Zackary made a stately statue. Crimson's energy had caught him in a moment of bravery, as a noble warrior. He had sacrificed himself to save his sister.

Ana felt a lump in her throat. She had underestimated her brother's courage. Crimson turned her malevolent gaze on Ana and stalked toward her.

"I'll get you—and your little dog!"

Ana hesitated. But if Crimson caught her now, her brother's sacrifice would have been for nothing. Courage was one thing, but wisdom was another.

"I'll be back!" Ana promised her brother. Then she turned and fled.

"I'm coming!" Veto scampered after her.

I will return and rescue my brother and Marilla, Ana vowed. *But I can only return if I can survive right now.*

Crimson shot a bolt of energy at Ana but missed. Dirt kicked up nearby as Ana sprinted away. Another shot whizzed by, narrowly missing Veto.

CHAPTER 34
PRINCE HUNTER

A high-tech hover motorcycle arrived. Without meaning to, the driver in a mirrored helmet got in the line of fire and gave Ana a chance to escape. A laser blast narrowly missed him.

"Hey! Hey! Don't shoot the messenger!"

"What do you want?" said Queen Crimson.

Bringing the hover bike to a stop beside Crimson, the driver lifted his visor, revealing Prince Hunter's handsome face for Crimson's eyes only.

"News flash—Opus Die turned down your planetary mining permit. He said we need to evacuate Avenir," said Prince Hunter.

"Never! We never got that message, understood?" snarled Queen Crimson. "Now do something useful for once. Don't let Zorana get to the portal. Head her off! Take that side." She pointed urgently at Ana's fleeing back.

Prince Hunter scowled as Queen Crimson turned on her heel. He flipped down his mirrored visor and jabbed a button.

But the hover bike refused to start.

CHAPTER 35
THE PORTAL

Thrusting her ice-cold hands into her pockets, Ana discovered the cookies. She did the only thing she could think of.

"Polly, want a cracker?" Ana rummaged noisily in her pocket, jiggling the broken pieces of cookie. Ana held up a morsel. "Polly, want a cracker?"

The parrot swooped toward Ana. She ran toward the open wardrobe door, Veto at her heels. The parrot flew after them, eager to claim the treat.

As Crimson didn't want to endanger her precious parrot, she couldn't risk shooting toward Ana. The helmeted stranger managed to start the recalcitrant hover bike and aimed it toward Ana.

"Mementomori, come back here," Crimson demanded.

The greedy parrot hesitated for a moment, then

obeyed. It flew back toward Crimson in a blur of red, yellow, and blue plumage.

"Come to me, Mementomori," Ana crooned. Although the very last thing Ana felt like doing was singing, she sang "Ana's Song." It had worked before. Could that be part of her charm as an animal whisperer?

But before it reached Crimson, the rebellious parrot banked and flew back toward Ana instead.

"No, no!" Crimson screamed in frustration as the defiant bird escaped her grasp.

Distracted, the biker glanced toward Crimson and was unseated as the hover bike bucked as it passed over a lichen-covered boulder. He landed with a thump on the frost-covered ground and groaned.

He peered up at Zackary's frozen body, gave a melodramatic sigh, and grumbled, "I hate frozen."

The hover bike continued zooming toward Ana, riderless. She leaped on it gleefully as it was heading in the right direction. *I'll make it to the portal twice as fast!*

Crimson clapped her hands twice, and the portal closed remotely. The light in the doorway died. Ana watched her chance to escape vanish as she zoomed toward the place the doorway had been.

How do I stop this thing? Where are the brakes? Hopeless with machinery, Ana pressed buttons, trying to find the brakes, but instead hitting the accelerator. She tumbled off it and rolled, as she had been taught to do in her parkour training. The hover bike carried on, then came to an abrupt stop when it smashed into a rock.

The helmeted stranger limped toward her and groaned, seeing the crumpled hover bike.

Ana discovered only a solid rock wall where the wardrobe had been. Her scrabbling fingers couldn't find any doorway. She kept slamming her shoulder into the stone wall but it didn't budge.

Whirling, she saw Crimson closing in on her, smiling vindictively. The helmeted stranger was closing in, too, and she'd be caught between them.

Ana needed the parrot to open the portal. Once again, she fished in her pocket, rustling the broken cookie. She held up a treat. "Polly, want a cracker?"

Ana sang, putting all her heart into it. The parrot veered toward Ana. The parrot was getting closer ... but so was Crimson.

Hurry up, hurry up, hurry up!

Crimson sped up, her steps thudding against the frozen earth. The biker hobbled faster, closing in on her.

Veto howled anxiously and clawed at the rock. "Predator!"

Ana frantically pounded on the rock wall that had once been a portal door. "Let me in! Let me in!"

Crimson's wicked smile flashed. "No one can hear you."

A chill of dread ran down Ana's spine. She threw her shoulder against the stone with all her might, but it remained immovable. The portal between worlds was closed.

Dread soured her stomach, and she tasted copper. In seconds, she would be at Crimson's mercy. And then there would be no hope for Zackary, Marilla, or Veto.

Come to me, Mementomori. Hurry!

Ana snapped her fingers twice. Just as all hope seemed lost, the parrot responded to this command and landed on Ana's shoulder with a whoosh of feathers.

Just as she had heard Crimson do earlier, Ana gave the command. "Apertus!"

Immediately, the rock wall shimmered, and the wardrobe appeared once again. Ana hurled herself through the wardrobe.

Crimson screeched in frustration as Ana, Veto, and her parrot escaped. Crimson sprang forward and grabbed the hem of the blue cloak.

CHAPTER 36
DIVAS

BLUEBELLS INN, PROSPERUS, TELLUSORA.

Inside the wardrobe, Ana's cloak throttled her as Crimson had hold of the hem. Ana undid the clasp, dropped the constraining cloak, and sprang free.

But Crimson was right behind her.

Ana whirled to shut the wardrobe door in Crimson's face. Her feet kicked Marilla's silver chain with the two master keys. She picked up the keys and fumbled to lock the wardrobe door, finally managing to do so.

But the locked door didn't stop Crimson. Her sharp red nails shredded through the thin door as if it were made of paper.

Crimson's arm flailed about, searching for her

prey, her sharp nails nearly skewering Ana. Ana leaped away, narrowly avoiding her scarlet claws.

"Apex predator," yelped Veto.

Fragments of wood splintered as Crimson slashed her way through the door.

"Come on, Veto!" Ana raced for the hallway, pulling the chain with the master keys over her head, finding it odd that she had dropped them the first time she went through the portal.

Ana burst out of room 33, followed by Veto and the parrot.

Tellusora was like a sauna and Ana began to sweat.

Ana careened into a man in the hallway. "Oh, sorry!"

"Watch where you're going!" the man complained as Ana dashed by. He was a slender man with gray hair, and he carried two struggling swans, one clamped firmly under each arm. The surly swans hissed and struggled to get free. "Kids and pets—the bane of my existence. Never again will I direct *Swan River*. Never again."

These swans were the stars of *Swan River*. In other words, divas! Not at all the elegant, sophisticated creatures one might imagine, but aggressive, ill-natured, and territorial. Ana assumed the man holding them was the Director.

A moment later, the parrot swooped into the hallway, following Ana. (Or, more accurately, following the cookies.) Chaos ensued as the Director lost his grip on the swans. The three large birds made a tremendous commotion, flapping, squawking, and hissing.

Veto barked and happily gave chase, increasing the pandemonium. The commotion upset some easily offended inn guests, who retreated into their rooms. Others with more resolve edged by the commotion, tutting with disapproval or smirking with amusement.

The Director chased his swans down the hallway. The flapping, honking birds shed white and orange feathers and left a trail of sticky white guano as they "lightened the load." The heavy swans flapped their wings energetically, but their clipped wingtips prevented them from gaining more than a foot of elevation.

Ana raced down the narrow hallway as feathers floated around her like dandelion fluff. She looked back over her shoulder and gasped in dismay to see Crimson in pursuit, her beautiful face dark with rage. No longer wearing her fur coat and hat, Crimson brushed splinters of wood off her red dress.

Oblivious, the Director tried to reclaim his swans. "Corner 'em!"

Ana only cared about getting as far away as possible..

"Come on, Veto!" Ana threw open the door at the end of the hallway. She dashed through it.

"Coming!" Veto scampered behind her.

The three birds followed, escaping the confines of the hallway. They honked triumphantly and flapped into the stairwell.

"Hey! What did you do that for?" said the Director.

Ana stumbled and fell down the stairs: it was painful, but fast. Thanks to her martial arts training, she knew how to tumble and roll. She picked herself up and flung open the door at the bottom, determined to escape. Veto ran at her heels. The stairs opened onto the restaurant, pub, and garden area. Patrons lounged, sipping drinks, nibbling sandwiches, and gossiping.

Dozens of eyes turned to see the spectacle of three large birds, one girl, and one dog, all being chased by the Director. Out of breath, Ana paused with her back to a pillar, hidden from the Director's view.

Where's Veto? She scanned the crowd but couldn't see the little dog.

Ana's image was reflected in the three Silver Screen mirrors recently installed, courtesy of the Crimson Censor. As a result, inn patrons could watch the show from multiple angles.

The Director chased his swans, but they eluded him, honking. Patrons laughed at the antics. Trying to make the best of an embarrassing situation, the Director announced, "Don't miss the show tonight! *Swan River!*"

Gasping to catch her breath, Ana hunted for a way

to escape. The cookies in her pocket rustled. The greedy parrot flew toward her and landed on her shoulder.

Beam me up, Scottie, Ana thought. *Wait a minute! What if I can open a portal right here and right now?*

Ana hissed, "Apertus!"

CHAPTER 37
ARRESTED

But nothing happened.

She thought, *Parrot's on my shoulder. That word had worked a minute ago. Take two!*

Ana repeated the spell, louder this time. "Apertus!"

To her dismay, reality didn't shift, and no portal opened. What was she missing? People regarded her strangely.

The parrot squawked, "If I want your opinion, I'll tell it to you."

Crimson arrived in the doorway, holding a single, long orange feather—evidence that her bird had flown this way.

Crimson's eyes swept the crowd, which hushed in anticipation. For a long moment, Crimson couldn't spot her prey. "Where is she?"

Betraying Ana, the magic mirror called out, "She's here!"

The Crimson Censor spotted Ana's reflection in the Silver Screen and strode toward her. Patrons craned to see the showdown.

The parrot squawked, "Resistance is futile."

"Thief!" Crimson accused, playing to the watching crowd. "Thief! She's got my bird."

The parrot perched on Ana's shoulder gave considerable weight to the accusation.

One fascinated patron told another, "We *must* get tickets to the show tonight. If this is any indication, it's going to be quite the spectacle!"

"By the power vested in me by Opus Die, I hereby place Zorana Zest under arrest. She's a murderer." The Crimson Censor clanged her burnished bracelets together with a reverberating ringing noise. Ana slipped around the pillar and the shot missed.

The distinctive ringing noise terrified those who had witnessed Mr. Berger's transformation into a wooden puppet. A frightened waiter dropped a tray of drinks. Glass shattered.

Spooked, the parrot took flight from Ana's shoulder—and then burst into flame. Ana recoiled.

The burning bird turned to bright embers. Patrons gasped in shock, mesmerized. The Silver Screens reflected the image multiple times, intensifying the display like fireworks.

You could count on the good people of Prosperus to enjoy a spectacle. Especially one that started with pyrotechnics.

"It caught on fire all by itself!" Ana protested. "I didn't do it!"

Cook had warned her to be careful, to blend in, not to attract attention. But now all eyes were on her. Her heart hammered and her mouth went dry. Just when she needed to be a brilliant actor, her wits abandoned her.

"Only a witch could incinerate a bird like that." Crimson pointed to the smoking remains of her parrot. Although honestly, the spontaneous combustion did a good job of drawing everyone's attention. Her comment merely underscored the obvious. For the benefit of those with limited vocabularies, the Crimson Censor added, "She burned it."

A blue feather wafted down toward the embers and ignited as it neared the hot coals. The beautiful blue feather blackened, shriveled, then turned to ash. Ana felt a pang of loss over the death of the parrot, who had been her friend, if only briefly.

A downy white feather floated lazily toward the same fate, held aloft by a gentle breeze. Without thinking, Ana rescued the feather from incineration and pocketed the memento of the late Mementomori.

"She's a witch!" Crimson's husky voice reverberated powerfully.

"No, I'm not. You are!" Ana said, but her voice sounded shrill and childish in comparison.

Is this a comedy? Like spectators at a tennis match, the onlookers turned to Crimson to see how she would return that lob.

"Like a schoolgirl. How original," Crimson said, dripping sarcasm. Then, remembering the simple-minded crowd, she dumbed it down. "A childish taunt—a childish reaction. You are under arrest." She drew herself up to her full height. She looked like a queen—possibly an evil one, but a queen nonetheless.

The spectators were awed by the status of the majestic and powerful Crimson Censor. Ana sensed she would never be able to get them on her side. It was like her worst nightmare: being onstage naked, with the entire audience mocking her.

Ana plowed on anyway. "You're a witch! You turned my brother to solid ice!"

The spectators gawked at Crimson. What next?

Crimson raised one perfect eyebrow. "People turned to ice? How ridiculous."

The more Ana tried to explain, the worse things got. She had no credibility in this drama. "You did! You turned Zackary and Marilla into ice statues."

Hearing Marilla's name, some people murmured with concern.

"In this heat?" Crimson scoffed. "Why would I

turn people into ice statues when wooden puppets are so much more useful?"

"Not here—in a parallel universe."

Patrons gasped, horrified that Ana dared to speak these forbidden words.

"Parallel universes do not exist," the Crimson Censor said, her husky voice growing even more dangerous. "Opus Die forbids spreading such vile lies. That's a Word Crime. Koercers!"

Mr. Berger, the gnarled wooden owner of Bluebells Inn, arrived accompanied by two of Crimson's Koercers. All three of them were men transformed into meek wooden puppets.

"What's going on?" barked Mr. Berger.

Crimson strode toward Ana and seized her wrist. For a split second, she seemed distracted by the fresh blood on Ana's arm, and her exquisite nostrils flared. Ana's skin crawled.

But then Crimson thrust Ana's wrist up high in the air so all could see. The three Silver Screens reflected the incriminating image of the cuff twinkling with tiny emeralds.

"She murdered the Emerald Censor. Here's the proof of it! She's wearing the Emerald Censor's cuffs." Crimson's voice was powerful and mesmerizing.

Patrons gaped at Ana with newfound respect. Crimson scowled at the onlookers, and they quickly concealed their astonishment that anyone—especially a girl—could kill a Censor.

The Koercers closed in and seized Ana. Their wooden faces were as lifeless as a stone gargoyle, devoid of emotion and yet threatening.

"By the power vested in me by Opus Die, I charge this witch with the worst crime of all—murdering a Censor!" declared Crimson.

Ana had never felt more alone. But suddenly she glimpsed Egor in a shadowed corner, unobserved by the inn guests. Egor silently clipped a leash to Veto's collar to prevent him from dashing toward Ana.

Veto watched Ana being arrested and whimpered, "Mango! Mango!"

Without so much as a friendly nod, Egor melted away, taking Veto with him.

At least Veto's safe. But is Egor on my side?

Ana tore her gaze from the pair so as not to betray their presence to the Censor, who would surely turn them both into wooden puppets if given half a chance.

Mr. Berger spotted Marilla's chain with the two master keys dangling from Ana's neck. "Hey, what's this? What are you doing with Marilla's keys?"

He yanked the chain from her neck in a fury. "Where's my daughter? If anything happened to her, you'll hang."

They dragged her away to prison.

CHAPTER 38
YOU'RE MY ONLY HOPE

The scene in the Manifester faded.
LORD ORATOR'S CASTLE, VERDANT, TELLUSORA.

Lord Orator and Ana looked up from the swirling images which had revealed the recent past. Now Lord Orator knew how Ana had arrived in Tellusora from London, England and ended up arrested, imprisoned, and then hanged. Thanks to the magical Manifester, he had seen everything Ana had seen.

"Well, that certainly explains how you earned the enmity of the Crimson Censor," said Lord Orator. "Most interesting."

Ana nodded, not trusting her swollen tongue or befuddled brain. So recently revived from being hanged within an inch of her life, she definitely was not at her best.

A small white-and-brown dog dozed by the fire in Lord Orator's office, and Egor hovered discreetly nearby.

"That was quite the neat trick, the way you eliminated the Emerald Censor." Lord Orator steepled his fingers thoughtfully.

"Thhee wath in the wrong place at the wrong time," lisped Egor.

"Or she was in the right place at the right time. It all depends on your point of view," Lord Orator said philosophically.

"It was an accident—that's just where the PUP landed. I didn't mean to kill her," Ana said.

"You didn't kill her. Evil entities such as that can never be taken off the board game permanently. Energy can neither be created nor destroyed. Her energetic essence has returned to wherever evil things go to regenerate. She'll be back ... but not for a long, long time."

"Oh."

"The Emerald Censor was a thorn in my side. So I owe you a debt of gratitude."

Unsure of what to say, Ana said nothing. She pushed a lock of white-blonde hair away from her stunning violet eyes. Her wrists were no longer adorned with the magical cuffs. "What happened to my golden cuffs? I mean, the ones from the Emerald Censor?"

"Egor removed them while you were unconscious."

"Can I have them back? Please?"

"No, of course not. I can't allow you to go about my world blasting things with a powerful weapon you don't know how to use, as I'm sure you can understand."

"Oh," Ana said, disappointed.

"I want to talk to you about magic. Are you curious about wizardry? Do you want to know how to command the world to do your bidding?" Lord Orator scrutinized Ana.

She had no interest in commanding the world to do her bidding. "I need to save my brother."

"That will be dangerous."

"I *have* to save Zackary. And Marilla too."

"An admirable, if naïve, sentiment."

"I can't leave them frozen and trapped in that place. Zackary sacrificed himself to save me."

"And you think sacrificing yourself as well will somehow make his sacrifice more meaningful?"

"No ... but ..." She dared not voice the bleak thought that her brother was already dead. Her voice quavered as she asked, "How long can he survive as a frozen statue?"

Lord Orator turned away, ambled to the window, and gazed outside pensively. "Fish can survive being frozen in ice in winter, then thaw and swim away in spring, unharmed. Egor, what's the estimated half-life of a human being in cryogenic suspension?"

Egor thought for a moment. "Difficult to thay, my Lord. It all dependth upon initial conditionth. There are too many variabelth to predict half-life with accuraty."

"What do you mean by half-life?" Ana asked shrilly. "I want him to have a whole life!"

"You're steadfast and true," Lord Orator observed, stroking his pointed black beard thoughtfully. "Half-life refers to the time required for half of something to undergo a process of disintegration or decay."

"That sounds awful. I don't want him to disintegrate or decay." Her nerves were shattered. Her hands trembled, and she dropped her cup, splashing hot tea on the floor and scalding herself. "Ow!"

Egor was there in a wink, mopping up the spill.

"How can I save him? And quickly?" Ana asked.

"You can't," said Lord Orator.

"But I have to! I have to go right now!"

"Then you will die. Foolishly and pointlessly. If you die, your brother dies, too. And Marilla Berger. No one else is going to save them," said Lord Orator.

"Every day—every minute—brings my brother closer to death." Ana's voice broke.

"Is that true?" Lord Orator mused philosophically.

Ana blurted, "I must get going!"

"Going where?"

"I've got to get back to Bluebells Inn. Go through the portal and rescue my brother!"

"How will you do that?"

That stumped Ana, and tears threatened to spill down her cheeks. She wiped them away angrily, determined to be brave and do the right thing. "I don't know. I'll think of something."

"Is that your best plan? Winging it?" Lord Orator said disdainfully.

"It's always worked before," Ana tried, mustering the last of her optimism.

"Is that true? Winging it seems to be the reason you and your brother are in so much trouble now."

His words were like a knife in her heart. Ana swallowed the lump in her throat.

He's right. This is all my fault. I need to find a way to fix it. But how?

Humbly, she asked, "Will you help me? Please?"

The question hung in the air for a long moment.

His back to her, Lord Orator continued gazing out the window. He sighed. "It won't be easy to go to Avenir, overcome the robots and the powerful Crimson Censor, thaw Zackary and Marilla, and bring them back alive ... with no training, supplies, or support team."

Ana felt an overwhelming wave of despair. "It sounds impossible when you put it that way. But I have to try."

"There is no 'try.' Only the weak *try*. The strong *do*. They stack the deck in their favor. Imagine what you could achieve with the proper training. You could fulfill the Prophecy." Lord Orator turned toward her, his clever eyes twinkling.

"The Prophecy?" Ana repeated, stupidly.

Lord Orator steepled his graceful fingers. "Let me see now. How does it go?"

Egor handed him a scroll. It was the kind of service few could afford. Apparently Glebs were trained to anticipate their master's needs and to give them what they needed before they even asked for it.

Ana blinked owlishly. *How does he do that?*

"Ah, yes. Thank you, Egor." Lord Orator unrolled the scroll and read in a musical voice,

> *Invaders will come from a land of twin sun,*
> *Our only hope is the Chosen One.*
>
> *Snowy hair, silver tongue, eyes lavender jewels,*
> *He'll free us all from oppressive rules.*
>
> *Born when the moon sets, rises, and is sky high.*
> *Unbeaten below unblinking eye,*

Masterverse, portal key, otherworldly
*   knight,*
He will break the ruthless tyrant's might.

Lord Orator rolled up the scroll and handed it back to Egor.

"I can't be the Chosen One. I don't have a silver tongue." Ana furrowed her brow. "And what use is a silver tongue anyway?"

"A silver tongue is just the thing to break cruel chains. Lies fuel evil. Evil cannot withstand the light of truth."

Ana blushed and fidgeted as Lord Orator studied her appraisingly.

He strolled over to contemplate a checkered game board. It resembled a chess set, but with trolls and hippogriffs and dragons, rather than pawns and knights and rooks. The finely carved marble pieces were scattered over the board, as he was apparently in the midst of playing a game.

Egor brought Ana a fresh cup of tea, and she sipped it, savoring the comforting, earthy scents of cinnamon, orange rind, and honey.

She soothed her frayed nerves by affirming, *Zackary is alive. Our mother's angel will protect him. I am guided in all things. Help comes from everywhere and everyone.*

As if contemplating a decision, Lord Orator mused,

"That Prophecy is why there's no one left alive your age with white hair and violet eyes. No one, that is—but you."

She mustered her courage. "I'm not the Chosen One. I'm not a boy, and I'm not a Masterverse—whatever that is. I couldn't possibly have been born when the moon was in three places simultaneously. I don't have any special powers—unfortunately—but I do need your help. I have to save Zackary. You're my only hope. Help me, Lord Orator."

Lord Orator toyed with the long, sharp scissors on his desk. "I don't believe in prophecies."

Ana blinked in surprise. "You don't?"

"No. I believe in action and information. I am curious about magic. And that is why I am willing to help you—but we have to do things *my* way. There'll be no rushing in like a fool. There will be planning and proper training. In other words, I am offering you a scholarship."

CHAPTER 39
THE CHOICE

"But I don't know anything about magic." Ana was getting dizzy, trying to follow Lord Orator's train of logic. She felt intellectually outmatched. If she was an amateur chess player, he was a master.

"Then it seems in alignment with learning something about it, now doesn't it?"

"But ... they sentenced me to die—"

"Miss *Zorana* was sentenced to die. And she did. Right, Miss *Ana*?"

"Right, right." Ana's head was swimming.

"Try to catch up. I don't offer apprenticeships to stupid people. You're still recovering from being hanged, so I'm going to give you a bit of latitude. Your tongue doesn't seem to be connected to your brain. So let me be clear. Your assignment is to become a student at the Academy, learn, and report back to me."

"You want me to be a spy?"

"A spy? No, no, no. We don't spy on our citizens and friends! We take an interest. Information is power. Lack of information is problematic. You will learn, and you will share what you have learned with me," Lord Orator replied.

"May I ask a question?"

"You just did," Lord Orator sighed, as this idiotic question was apparently one of his pet peeves. He had little tolerance for imprecise communication. "Yes, you may ask *another* question."

"What about my brother? Is he ... is he ... d-d-dead?" She stumbled over the dreaded word. "His last words were 'I'm a goner anyway'—is that true?"

"Good question, but I think he was referring to his illness. The worst things can be the best things, if you're willing to look for the hidden gift. Cryogenic suspension may be precisely the thing needed to kill cancer."

"Do you think so?" Ana twisted the lace sleeve of her dress anxiously, barely daring to hope. *How does he know about Zackary's cancer?*

"Rescuing him is a task far beyond your skills. At least far beyond your *current* skills. Hence, training is absolutely necessary. Perhaps you can learn how to fulfill your potential as an apprentice under the Wizard Snapdragon."

"The Wizard Snapdragon?" Ana perked up, hope dawning like a sunrise in her heart. She wanted to meet the person who could heal her brother. "The famous Wizard Snapdragon who can heal anyone of anything?"

"So I've heard. Good luck is when preparedness meets opportunity. I can provide the opportunity. The rest is up to you."

Torn between self-doubt and the need to rescue her brother, Ana chewed her lip anxiously.

"In the final analysis, I want information. You want to learn how to get back to Avenir, save your brother, and return to Earth. So you need to find the portal keys to parallel universes. Does the Wizard Snapdragon have a portal key? Can you, ahh ... *liberate* that portal key?"

"*Steal*, you mean."

"So direct, so crude, so vulgar." Lord Orator sniffed disapprovingly. "Try to acquire a degree of style. Shall we say *borrow* ... for an indefinite period?"

"But I'm not a thief."

"Uh-uh-uh," he tutted. "So slow to catch on."

"I'm not a ... *borrower*?"

"I prefer *liberator*."

"I like liberator. It sounds more like a rescuer than a thief."

"Isn't that more accurate?"

"Well ... I do want to liberate my brother and Marilla."

"Exactly. And you'll need a portal key to pull that off."

"True. But I'm not a spy."

"Details, details! You're an actress. The difference between an actress and a spy is the minor detail that you report back to me. Think of it as improv."

Lost at sea, Ana found a raft of hope to cling to. "I am pretty good at improv."

"Excellent. Our interests are aligned. Win-win. I help you, and in exchange, you report what you learn back to me. And bring me any item you *liberate*. You can keep your brother and the little girl, of course," Lord Orator said. "Why not consider it the role of a lifetime?"

"The role of a lifetime," Ana mused. Hope arose like a warm sunset in Venice Beach, California, water shimmering brightly on the surface ... even though the ocean could contain sharks lurking in hidden depths.

These were the thrills she lived for! To dance on the edge. To channel all her creativity into convincing the audience. And, just like in live theater, there were no second chances. She could never break character, never betray fear. She had no bandwidth to yearn for a mother, wonder why her father hated her, or feel that she didn't belong anywhere. When she was acting, she felt alive and euphoric.

"The Wizard Snapdragon is rumored to have a multiverse map. If she does, it would be more valuable than my entire estate. Is that true? Can you liberate it?"

"Is this why you saved me from hanging?"

"It's one of the reasons."

"Would you mind telling me the other reasons?"

"Yes."

Ana waited, but Lord Orator didn't elaborate.

"And those other reasons are ... ?"

"Yes, I *would* mind telling you those other reasons," Lord Orator clarified. "Really, such imprecise communication. What do they teach you in school these days? Pay attention."

"And—hypothetically speaking—what happens if I say no to your generous offer of a scholarship?" said Ana.

"You can walk out that door. There is always a choice. But you will never see me—or your brother—again," warned Lord Orator. "It's your choice."

Where would I go? How can I rescue my brother by myself? How can I evade the Crimson Censor with no friends or resources?

"Not much of a choice," murmured Ana.

"But a choice nonetheless," Lord Orator said. "I believe in free will. Not everyone does, as you know.

Free will and free enterprise. The pillars of a thriving city."

"Um ..."

"I do warn you. This is a onetime offer. And it expires in one minute. If you don't accept, I will award this scholarship to another promising candidate. So ... what do you choose?"

CHAPTER 40
THE RELUCTANT SPY

"In that case, I'm off to see the Wizard," Ana said brightly.

Lord Orator raised an eyebrow.

"I'm pleased to accept your offer, Lord Orator," said Ana.

"Excellent. Continue capturing the essence of your adventures in your notebook." Lord Orator took her journal out of his desk drawer and gave it to her. "I found your story most ... refreshing."

"You read my journal?" Ana blushed and clutched her precious journal to her chest.

"Try not to lose it again. We would not want it falling into the wrong hands. Of course, most people could not read it, and even if they could, they would think it a fanciful fairy tale."

"But it's all true!"

"Yes, I know." Lord Orator brushed her protest aside. "Brightness Cacophony—otherwise known as the Crimson Censor—will stop at nothing to find you and eliminate you. Now that you know her secret, you are a danger to her. Right now, she believes you are dead. She saw Miss Zorana Zest hang, as did a hundred other witnesses. It would be best if she continued to believe that you are dead. Otherwise, the Crimson Censor will become extremely hazardous to your health."

Ana nodded. *That's an understatement.*

"Best go by Ana from now on. And best to choose another last name. What name would you like?"

Ana blurted the first name that popped into her head. "How about Taylor?"

"Fine. Ana Taylor it is. And don't mention portals or parallel universes or the existence of the multiverse. Opus Die has outlawed these ideas." Lord Orator straightened the letter opener on his desk so that it was aligned and spaced evenly with his in-tray and scissors.

"How can you outlaw ideas?"

"By declaring them treason. Which entirely misses the point of thinking. We think so that our thoughts can die—rather than us. Thinking is useful," mused Lord Orator, toying with the silver scissors on his desk. "However, your more immediate concern is the Academy entrance exam."

"What kind of entrance exam?"

"I'm sure Dr. Jordan Verity will have devised something clever to sort the pearls from the pretenders. If you fail the entrance exam, then I am mistaken about you. I don't like to be wrong. I will not interfere again with local justice."

Ana gulped and touched her tender throat. It sounded like a failing grade would cause another appointment with the hangman. "Who is Dr. Jordan Verity?"

"He's the headmaster at the Academy."

"But won't I get in trouble for learning magic? Isn't that a crime punishable by death?"

"That is regrettably true—as long as Opus Die remains in power."

"Is there an election coming up soon?"

Lord Orator scoffed. "Opus Die hates elections even more than magic. No one can challenge his 'divine rule.' No elections, no votes, no veto."

At his name, the lapdog dozing by the fire awoke and gazed at Lord Orator expectantly, then limped over to nuzzle his master.

Lord Orator frowned, apparently irritated by his dog's odd gait. "You're my daily reminder of the value of veto power. It works imperfectly—like you, Veto." He patted the dog fondly, but with a hint of distaste.

"Veto! You're all right!" Ana cried. "I was so worried about you!"

"I was worried about you," Veto barked.

Ana peered at Lord Orator to see if he had understood, but he gave no such sign. *But his face is inscrutable, so I can't be sure.*

Veto scampered toward her, leaping in a frenzy of excitement onto her lap. His little body trembled with joy, and he showered her with wet doggy kisses. Ana enveloped him in her arms, and he snuggled into her embrace, his creamy white-and-brown fur radiating warmth. He let out a blissful sigh. Ana stroked his silky ears affectionately.

"Can I take Veto with me?"

"*May* I," corrected Lord Orator. He observed their connection thoughtfully. "Many students with magical abilities have an animal familiar. Very well."

"Want to come with me, Veto?" Ana asked.

He wagged his tail and barked, "Take me! Take me! I'm your secret protector and lie detector!"

Ana glanced at Lord Orator, but his face betrayed nothing. She seemed to be the only one who understood Veto. Ana crooned affectionately, "Who's a good boy?"

"I am! I am!" Veto barked, pleased with all the attention.

"Is there any way to get word to my Dad and Uncle Shockley? They'll be worried about me and Zackary. Can we send them an email or something?"

"An email." Lord Orator snorted. "How quaint. I

think you have failed to grasp the concept of the multiverse. Each world is disconnected from every other world. Unless you have the right portal key. If you want to send a message back home, you'll have to deliver it yourself, in person."

Ana chewed her lip. She was stuck here. And what would she say anyway, even if she could email? *Zackary and I are fine. We're having a bit of a holiday in the multiverse. We made a few friends and some powerful enemies. Zackary is frozen in another world. But it's not a problem, so don't worry. I'm going to rescue Zackary, and we'll be back in time for supper.* That would be a stretch, and who would believe such a strange message, anyway?

Ana shifted her attention back to the Academy. "Learning magic is a crime?"

"Unfortunately, people have such a regrettable tendency to react with fear—rather than curiosity—to things they do not comprehend. Don't make that mistake, Ana. Greater understanding can never make you worse off. See what you can learn and discern. Then report back to me, using one of these."

Lord Orator slid open a drawer in his desk and pulled out a velvet-lined box. He plucked out a silver orb the size of an egg.

"The Gossipfly Mark II. Delightful invention. I get the latest gadgets—it's a benefit of being a patron of the arts. This one has twice the range of the Mark I."

Lord Orator admired the device. "You simply speak your message into the Gossipfly Mark II and release it. It will fly back to me and deliver your message. Like this."

He activated the Gossipfly Mark II by pressing his thumb on the pointy end of the egg. It unfolded and expanded into a large dragonfly-like device. Then he whispered a message into it and gently tossed it aloft.

The Gossipfly flew to Ana and did a facial recognition scan to confirm her identity. Then it blew an enormous pink bubble around her head. Inside the bubble, she heard Lord Orator's voice. "I'll only be able to retrieve your message once, so be sure to enunciate clearly. Don't mumble. Articulate clearly!"

Message delivered, the pink bubble popped like bubble gum. Veto barked, startled, and leaped from Ana's lap. He frantically pawed at the sticky pink substance on his whiskers, hilarious in his antics to get it off.

With distaste, Ana wiped a droplet of pink moisture from her face. The Gossipfly transformed back to its dormant egg form and lay in her palm.

"Egor will pack three Gossipflies in your belongings. Use them wisely. Tell me what you learn about magic and the multiverse. Does the Wizard Snapdragon know how to access other worlds? Does she have a portal key? What magic powers does she command? Can she truly heal anyone of anything?"

Veto perked up at Lord Orator's words. He barked, "Can she heal my leg?"

Ana paused to see if Lord Orator would answer Veto. When he didn't, she asked, "Can she heal Veto's leg?"

"You tell me," said Lord Orator.

"Can the Wizard give me a new heart?" Egor wondered.

"What's wrong with your heart?" Lord Orator asked.

"It's too thmall for true love," Egor confessed with a sigh. "No Gleborina will have me."

"Yet another question our spy may answer." Lord Orator strolled to the door of his office. "Goodbye and good luck, Ana. Veto come along now. Time for walkies."

Veto limped after his master, his feathery white tail wagging as it curled over his back. Ana wished Veto would stay with her. His presence was comforting.

Lord Orator paused at the doorway. "We are left only with the matter of radically altering your appearance. Egor, take care of it."

"Conthider it done, my lord."

Lord Orator exited, Veto reluctantly following at his heels. The door shut with a decisive thunk. Suddenly, Ana felt abandoned, small, and vulnerable.

Ana was alone with Egor. He reminded her of

Frankenstein, with his skin criss-crossed with stitches, a strangely rectangular head, and oily black hair. She felt a wave of dread as she gazed at him. What did she really know about the ways of Glebs?

Egor snapped on black rubber gloves and mixed something foul-smelling in a small cauldron. Fumes accosted Ana's nostrils.

"What's that horrible stench?" she asked.

Suddenly, straps sprouted from the arms of the torturer's chair and wrapped around her wrists, binding her.

Ana gasped. "Hey! Hey! What're you doing?"

"Radically altering your appearance," Egor said gleefully.

Grinning like a madman, he closed in on her, shiny scissors in one hand and the vile-smelling cauldron in the other.

"How about ... a sensational scar down your cheek?" Egor offered, as if this was the ultimate fashion statement.

"No, don't! I'll never make it in Hollywood! Can't we talk about this?"

"Lord Orator'th orderth are nonnegotiable." Egor loomed over Ana, flourishing the razor-sharp scissors like a rapier. "It'th for your own good."

"You're scaring me!" Ana yanked against the straps, but they held firmly.

Egor cackled insanely and started radically altering her appearance.

A NOTE FROM THE AUTHOR

Book reviews are the lifeblood of authors. If you liked this book, please take five seconds to leave a starred review online. That will let me know you'd like to read more books about Ana and Zackary's adventures in the multiverse.

Reviews are appreciated wherever you get books, such as Amazon, Bookbub, and Goodreads. Thank you very much!

To thank you for your time, a bonus chapter from the next book in this series follows.

BOOK 2: THE SECRET MULTIVERSE ACADEMY (BONUS CHAPTER)

The entrance exam for the Secret Multiverse Academy took place at a circus. Apparently, the headmaster thought the best place to do something clandestine was in a crowd.

Determined to find and destroy all freedom fighters, the Crimson Censor forced everyone to gather in the main circus tent.

Ana hid in the back row with her loyal lapdog, Veto, anxious to remain undetected.

The Crimson Censor lectured the audience about the importance of conformity and drove home her point by maliciously turning all the dogs into identical golden labs.

That's where we pick up the story ...

THE CIRCUS, PROSPERUS, TELLUSORA.

As Ana watched in horror, Veto morphed from a cute lapdog into a surprised golden lab. Caught in a world turned upside down, Ana pushed the suddenly heavy dog off her lap.

She glanced at the Crimson Censor, who was gloating in the spotlight on center stage, proud of her magical transformation of all the dogs into golden labs.

Stunned and outraged pet owners were seated in the rows in front of Ana. The elegant owner of an elegant red setter cried out in protest. The burly owner of a bullmastiff arose, spluttering with rage to see his hound turned into a golden lab. He instinctively reached for the knife on his belt, then thought better of it.

Veto collapsed on the floor, making choking sounds. His brown eyes bulged. The tiny collar was strangling him!

Fear gripped Ana as she struggled to unbuckle Veto's too-small collar. If she couldn't get the collar off, he would die! It dug deep into his flesh, buried in rolls of fur.

Veto frantically tried to claw the collar off with one hind leg, scratching her. Ana fought to unbuckle the collar, but Veto writhed about, making it impossible.

His brown eyes pleaded for help. He needed air! His pink tongue lolled out of his mouth.

Ana couldn't unbuckle the collar, though she tried with all her might. It was too tight.

Veto's eyes rolled back in his head. He slumped in a lifeless heap.

Ana gasped in horror. *No, no, no!*

Spotting the knife on the bullmastiff owner's belt, Ana grabbed it and slashed Veto's collar. Veto gasped, inhaling the air hungrily.

"Thanks." Ana handed the knife back to the burly man.

He nodded sternly, then whirled to confront the Crimson Censor. "I don't want a pet!" he bellowed. "I need a guard dog. Put my dog back in his proper form!"

As soon as he said these mutinous words, the Koercer troopers closed in, clattering as they moved. Once human, the Koercers had been transformed into puppet slaves. Their wooden faces were as blank and expressionless as a polished mahogany tabletop.

Hiding, Ana kneeled on the floor beside Veto as they arrested the burly man for Word Crimes. Veto gradually revived and gazed at her with gratitude.

Ana risked glimpsing up through the seats between her and the center stage, where Crimson was lecturing the audience.

Crimson quoted another slogan. "If I want your opinion, I'll tell it to you."

Enraged, Ana wondered how many dogs had just

died from strangulation. Angry thoughts crowded her head.

Crimson could have warned them if she had a heart. But she didn't—she's evil. Will people be next? Would Crimson transform them all into identical beings? What does a "standard girl" look like on Tellusora? Certainly not a violet-eyed Earthling like me!

Outraged, some people protested. Others held their tongues, cowed. Koercers descended upon the dissenters, arresting them one by one, extinguishing their voices of resistance.

The predatory smile on Crimson's face made it clear there would be no mercy. And the dire consequences of speaking up paralyzed the crowd.

Ana knew she had to act swiftly to escape. If the Crimson Censor somehow recognized her in spite of Egor's handiwork, Ana would hang—again. Her mind raced as she scanned the area for a way out. The chaos and confusion provided a small window of opportunity.

Koercers flanked the exits. Ana watched in the large Silver Screen as they detained the elegant woman, now the not-so-proud owner of a discombobulated golden lab.

With a determined glint in her eyes, Ana slipped into the shadows at the rear of the tent. Veto slunk after her, his tail between his golden legs.

"Long live Opus Die," commanded the Crimson Censor as she paced on stage in the spotlight.

"Long live Opus Die!" the audience obediently chanted, the chorus rising as they repeated the familiar refrain, "Long live Opus Die! Long live Opus Die!"

Ana couldn't stand it for one more minute. "Let's get out of here, Veto," she whispered.

Now a bewildered golden lab, Veto trailed behind her. As she crouched down behind the last row of seats, Ana slipped on her invisibility hat and vanished. Veto blinked in surprise, cocked his head quizzically, and sat down.

Ana squirmed out underneath the canvas tent wall, the refreshing scent of sawdust filling her nostrils as she crawled along. She arose outside the main tent in a narrow, shaded alleyway between circus tents.

Thanks to her invisibility hat, no one could see her. But if anyone had been watching, they would have seen the sawdust she brushed from her clothes appear in midair. It fell to the ground with a gentle patter. She breathed a sigh of relief, assuming she was safe.

But she was wrong about that.

An old lady carrying a large tapestry purse turned into the narrow alleyway between tents.

Two Koercer guards chased her. "Stop!"

Ana drew back and froze. She was invisible, but the

sound of her footsteps or breathing would betray her presence.

The crone calmly faced the Koercers. "Whatever for?"

"Inspection!"

The old lady's voice rippled with magical power. "I've got nothing to hide."

One of the Koercers grabbed her large tapestry purse and pawed through it. Coins clinked as he pocketed them.

The old lady remained unperturbed. "I don't have what you're looking for."

Mesmerized, one said, "She doesn't have what we're looking for."

"Get cracking," the crone said in a mesmerizing voice. "Chop-chop!"

"Get cracking," one repeated, hypnotized. "Chop-chop!"

The two Koercers let her go and moved along to hunt elsewhere.

The crone stared at Ana, arched an eyebrow, and stepped toward her.

Ana's breath hitched. *Did the invisibility hat stop working?* She took a step away, and gravel crunched underfoot.

The crone said, "Be still now."

Suddenly, the Crimson Censor arrived in the

narrow alleyway between circus tents. Ana held her breath.

"Idiots! Find the key!" Crimson said.

The Koercers snapped out of their daze. One patted down the crone. He found an ivory pendant on a chain concealed under her clothes. "Oho! What's this?"

"That's it!" Crimson eyed the ivory pendant greedily.

"That's not what you're searching for." The crone's voice reverberated with magical energy. She retrieved the pendant, a spiral horn wrapped with threads of silver and gold.

The Koercers again fell under the spell of her voice. But Crimson was immune to the old woman's magic.

"Arrest her!" Crimson strode toward the crone—and toward Ana.

Ana's stomach turned to acid. She wished she'd never snuck out of the circus tent. She hadn't avoided the Crimson Censor by sneaking out. And if Crimson discovered her, it would mean her death. She was in more danger now than ever!

To make matters worse, Veto started shimmying his way out from underneath the circus tent. His acute sense of smell led him right to the place where she stood, although she was invisible. Her heart pounded as Veto bounded eagerly towards her, drawing Crimson's eye. He would reveal her location any second!

"No, Veto! Go back," Ana hissed.

THANK you for leaving a book review online. I appreciate it very much. You'll help others discover an award-winning fantasy series.

To read the next chapters in book 2 and receive exclusive **Magic, Mystery and the Multiverse** bonus content, please join my mailing list. Get the multiverse maps, "sneak peeks" of the next chapters, and be the first to know about upcoming events, Kickstarter campaigns, and special editions. Benefit from early access to everything! I love hearing from my readers and when you join my community, it makes this more of a conversation. Your invitation is here: www.AuroraWinter.com/magic.

Don't miss out! Read the rest of the **Magic, Mystery and the Multiverse** series by Aurora M. Winter.

Magic, Mystery and the Multiverse 2: The Secret Multiverse Academy.

Acknowledgments

I deeply appreciate all the early readers who helped me shape this book and make it better. Their feedback fueled me with enthusiasm as I worked through multiple drafts for two years. Early readers asked important questions. Their input resulted, for example, in Veto playing a larger role. They let me know they enjoyed the story and the characters.

All of it made a difference to my journey writing this book, a book I've held in my heart and wanted to write for decades, ever since I read the Narnia series by C. S. Lewis.

As this is my first novel, the encouragement was especially valuable. Even though I'm an award-winning screenwriter and nonfiction author, writing fiction challenged me in new ways. It made a difference to have people who believed in me and were eager to read the next books in this series.

Thank you to my alpha readers, many of whom generously and patiently read multiple drafts of this book, including Danielle Chritchley, Timothy Forner,

Vera Huber, Andrea Viner, and Bryce Winter. My sincere appreciation goes to my team of beta readers, including Addie Davies, Clair Davies, Ro Davies, Christine Martin, Shondra Martin, and Wendy Winter. Squamish youth voted on the best title, and *Magic, Mystery and the Multiverse* was the winner.

I appreciate Aubrey Clarke from the BBC for his interest in creating a TV series, and for his suggestion that Uncle Shockley's house be located in England. I had fun making that change prior to this book's official publication.

My son, Yale Winter, created the wonderful maps of Tellusora and Avenir. Artistic author photos were created by the talented photographer Jana Marcus. I'm grateful for the eagle eyes of my editor, Amanda Bidnall. Award-winning cover art was created by Trif at TrifBookDesign.com.

Scrivener, ProWritingAid, and Vellum helped me improve this book. Any remaining errors are mine alone.

I stand upon a mountain of books by authors who have inspired and influenced me as a writer and as a human being. While the complete list would fill another book, I'd like to acknowledge a few great authors specifically: C. S. Lewis, J. R. R. Tolkien, L. Frank Baum, J. K. Rowling, Patrick Rothfuss, Brandon Sanderson, Philip Pullman, Norton Juster, and Sir

Terry Pratchett. If you want to become a writer, read voraciously!

Thank you, everyone! Know that I cherish your contributions, time, and support. You made a difference.

Aurora M. Winter

Aurora M. Winter is an award-winning author and screenwriter-producer.

Aurora loves teaching and inspiring people of all ages, and shedding light on issues that matter, including creative self-expression, literacy, free speech, and the environment.

Aurora divides her time between Vancouver, BC and Los Angeles, California and is a dual citizen of Canada and the United States.

A popular speaker, Aurora is frequently featured on podcasts and other broadcasts. She is the founder of SamePagePublishing.com.

Get your ***Magic, Mystery and the Multiverse*** bonus content here:
www.AuroraWinter.com/magic

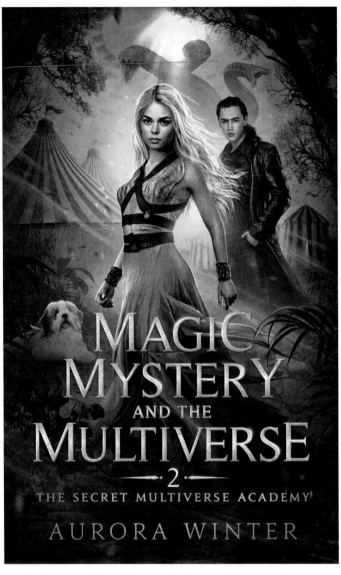

Magic, Mystery and the Multiverse 2: The Secret Multiverse Academy
by Aurora M. Winter

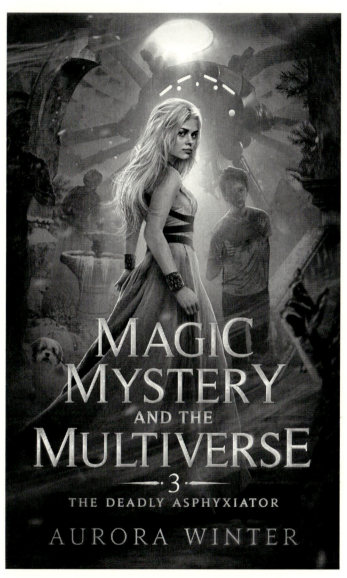

Magic, Mystery and the Multiverse 3: The Deadly Asphyxiator by
Aurora M. Winter

Manufactured by Amazon.ca
Acheson, AB